He turned, and the half smile left his face

The breath caught in her throat. It was as if her whole life had been leading up to this moment—the recognition of a stranger who was not a stranger at all.

He moved forward, his eyes never leaving hers, and she knew what he was silently asking, wanting. She knew that if he kissed her now she would respond with all the wanton ardor of a passionate nature long denied love.

"Tiah..." The controlled harshness of his voice shocked her. "Tiah, I'm offering you friendship, respect. Just that. I'll be honest—I hope friendship will develop into something more. But until you're ready for that something more to grow, I won't force the issue. And that's a promise."

He dragged in a long, harsh breath. "Now it's up to you. Take it or leave it!"

Diana Hamilton creates high-tension conflict that brings new life to traditional romance. Readers will no doubt find her a welcome addition to the Harlequin program and will be glad to know that more novels by this talented author are already in the works.

Books by Diana Hamilton

HARLEQUIN PRESENTS
993—SONG IN A STRANGE LAND

HARLEQUIN ROMANCE
2865—IMPULSIVE ATTRACTION

Dark Charade

Diana Hamilton

Harlequin Books

TORONTO • NEW YORK • LONDON
AMSTERDAM • PARIS • SYDNEY • HAMBURG
STOCKHOLM • ATHENS • TOKYO • MILAN

Original hardcover edition published in 1987
by Mills & Boon Limited

ISBN 0-373-HRS 11

Harlequin Romance first edition April 1988

Printed in U.S.A.

CHAPTER ONE

THE whispering began at teatime. A shiver crawled over Tiah's skin and her slender body stiffened, a taut expression sharpening her liquid grey eyes as she tilted her head, pinning down the faint but persistent sound.

Claudia's soft voice seemed to permeate the whole house . . . whispering . . . whispering . . .

Tiah uncoiled her long legs from the window seat where she had been sitting for the past hour, watching the graceful dip and soar of swallows above the placid sliding waters of the stream. The house, gracious and lovely as anything ever built by man from stone, had become, just for this moment in the slow-moving day, an uneasy place, filled with the sad drift of memories, with thoughts made real and somehow tangible by the soft persuasion of Claudia's voice.

She would go back to her studio, a wooden-frame building apart from the main house, get back to work and leave Claudia to her ghosts. Claudia was a dear, and Tiah loved her as she might have loved her own mother—had she ever been allowed to know her—but some things, these intense whispered conversations with her brother Oliver, a year dead but never for one moment forgotten, were aspects of Claudia's character Tiah could not feel easy about.

Tiah could not accuse her sister-in-law of holding seances. There was nothing ritualistic about the whispered conversations which Claudia, from time to time, directed towards the shade of Tiah's dead husband. And Claudia, older than Tiah by twenty years, was so marvellous in all other ways that Tiah didn't have the heart to upbraid her too rigorously for something that seemed to bring the older woman so much relief, even if it made Tiah herself feel desperately uncomfortable.

Three years ago Oliver had brought her here, to Deepdene, the sequestered stone house, isolated in its own valley in the richly timbered Shropshire hills, to meet his family. But his sister Claudia, fifteen years his senior, was the only family he had left. She had cared for him, with unselfish devotion, since their parents had died—his father before he had been born and his mother when he'd been little more than a toddler.

Claudia had welcomed Tiah, and had enveloped her with quiet, supportive affection when, four months later, Oliver had brought her home to Deepdene as his bride.

And after Oliver's death, just over a year ago, Claudia's undemanding and considerate support, her strength, had helped Tiah through the worst patch of her twenty-one years.

Claudia's grief over the loss of the younger brother she had made her whole life must have been intense, but she had kept it hidden inside her. She, mother-figure that she had by then become to the shy motherless Tiah, had sublimated her own misery and had found a quiet strength from somewhere to give to the tragic young widow.

So although Tiah worried she could hardly raise more than token objections when Claudia sometimes resorted to these eerie, whispered conversations because, this apart, life as Claudia had helped to make it was now pleasantly undemanding, easy, something that could be coped with, where pain was a stranger, only dimly remembered, glimpsed sometimes, but rarely now, in dreams that were grotesque enough to be dismissed as mental ravings in the clear light of day.

As Tiah slipped through the cool dim hall Claudia's whispering sounded louder, an uneasy counterpoint to the ruminative ticking of the brass-faced grandfather clock. Tiah let herself out of the front door, reaction sending a violent physical tremor through her as the blessed normality of the rays of the early summer sun struck through the oyster silk bloused top and matching loosely gathered skirt she wore.

Calmed by the wholesomeness of the combined scents of water, lush grass and flowering shrubs—the lilac and viburnum that Claudia had planted in her youth—Tiah wandered down the sloping bank to the edge of the stream, fascinated as always by the play of light and shade on the smooth surface of the water, the oily mysterious greenness where it slid beneath the old stone bridge.

Work could wait, and that was a luxury she owed both to Oliver and Claudia. Inherited wealth had meant that Oliver had never had to work for a living. But his painting had been his work, his all-consuming passion, and if his canvases hadn't sold, it hadn't mattered. Commercialism, he had often told her, had never needed to come between him and his art.

And Tiah herself had taken painting as her hobby, using watercolour where Oliver had worked in oils. It had been a way to fill in time. During the early days of her marriage she had talked about finding a job. At first, both her husband and sister-in-law had viewed her attempts to find employment with amused tolerance—rather in the way parents might smilingly watch a young child pretend to drive the family car—twisting the steering wheel with fierce concentration and making brum-brum noises, going absolutely nowhere.

It had been when Tiah had actually landed a job as a general dogsbody in a florist's shop in Compton, the nearest town of any size, that the real objections had been raised.

Oliver wanted her here, at home, with him. He didn't like the idea of her having to drive the twenty-odd miles into town and back each day, particularly in treacherous weather conditions; it was all so unnecessary.

But it had been Claudia who had finally won the day, gently pointing out that if Tiah took the job, not needing the money it would bring in, she would be depriving someone else of a useful wage packet. In days of record unemployment it had been an argument that Tiah, in all conscience, couldn't refute.

And so painting had become her hobby, something by which, eventually, she had been able to earn money she could call her own, and, after Oliver's death, a way of saving sanity, occupying her hands and her mind, leaving less time for painful memories.

Memories . . . She turned swiftly, as if something unpleasant were breathing over her shoulder, her high-heeled sandals gouging out a sliver of smooth green turf, her slippery ash-blonde hair swirling, silver in the sunlight, before settling back to her shoulders. She walked quickly up the incline, heading for her studio and the amnesiac properties of work.

At the top of the slope she paused, listening to the sound of an approaching car along the lane which looped the hollow where Deepdene lay. The narrow track led nowhere, except to the house, and very few people came this way apart from the occasional delivery van and Polly who drove out from the village each day to clean and cook.

But Polly was in the kitchen and they were expecting no deliveries today, so the approaching stranger had to be lost. It happened sometimes.

A slight frown ruffled her high smooth forehead, narrowing her long silvery grey eyes; there was nothing hesitant in the way the low, metallic blue car was being driven as it appeared on the brow of the hill, cornering smoothly to take the steep drive down to the house, crossing the stone bridge and pulling to a gravel-spattering halt on the wide forecourt fronting the house. And the stranger who eased his considerable length out of the driving-seat didn't look in the least way lost. He looked as if he always knew where he was going.

She moved out of the dappled shade afforded by the lilacs, a tall slim figure in the oyster silk that almost matched her hair for colour, her nearly beautiful features cast in the mould of serenity that had been won with so much difficulty since Oliver's death and which was now habitual.

The stranger had his back to her and was staring up at the house, and that didn't surprise her because Deepdene was beautiful. What did surprise her was the unplaceable sensation of panic that fluttered quickly inside her, catching at her throat, as her eyes made a sweeping assessment of him. Tall and well built—but not heavily so—very dark hair, crisp, cut short, a light grey suit that looked superbly tailored . . .

A breath of a breeze ruffled the warm air, carrying an unhurried drift of scent from the heavy blossoms, so that as she silently approached him she felt as if she were a creature of the perfumed air, cast adrift and set apart, somehow, from the realities of human contact. And he turned, suddenly, as if sensing her presence, and the small sensation of panic which she hadn't been able to put a name to, or explain away with reasoned logic, intensified unbearably as she met incredibly blue eyes, blackly fringed, in a face that was rugged planes and angles, attractively put together, smiling.

He took a couple of steps towards her, sure of himself, the blue eyes warm, the tanned skin crinkling a little at the corners as if he were used to smiling often, had come to terms with life and found it good. And Tiah's feet instinctively stopped, as if her body reacted to a danger her mind was incapable of comprehending.

'Mrs Paradine? Tiah Paradine?'

She nodded, foolishly tongue-tied as she took his outstretched hand. Instinctively, she withdrew her hand almost before proper contact had been made, and as her fingertips trailed across his palm she tightened her lips at the sensation of resurging panic which brought hot colour to her cheeks.

'Lucas Clent—proprietor and managing editor of the *Compton Gazette*. I'd like to talk to you about your work—if you can spare me half an hour?'

Nothing off-key about the request. Unusual, but not unnatural. So why did her wretched pulses suddenly accelerate with a rush of adrenalin, as if something threatened her?

She pasted a smile on her face and hoped it was

polite and hid what she really and unaccountably felt—that she didn't want to talk to him about anything, any time—and did her best to look interested.

Difficult to simulate interest in a paper she had hardly ever read since, for some reason, Claudia refused to have it in the house.

'My secretary tried to arrange an appointment by phone, but it appeared your line was out of order,' he offered and Tiah continued to smile, rather thinly she feared, knowing that Claudia often deliberately left the phone off the hook when she was in one of her solitary moods.

Lucas Clent hadn't moved closer, but Tiah still had the feeling he was crowding her. Every nerve-end suddenly seemed alive, and she didn't like that. And it was absurd, because he wasn't crowding her at all. Acquaintances, strangers, touched her life occasionally, and then passed on, forgotten in a moment, faceless, never reaching her. No one got near her now. It was better so. Much easier. Not that she consciously tried to give anyone the cold shoulder. It was within her, a cool remoteness, a self-sufficiency that inevitably formed a barrier around her which was as tangible as the highest, most heavily guarded wall.

With an effort she made herself move, assume a veneer of co-operation.

'Of course. Perhaps we'd better go to the studio.' Better not invite him to the house. Claudia was in a strange mood, had been all day, and the whispering, the eerie conversations with a man over a year dead, had been the culmination, an unwelcome recurrence of something Tiah had hoped was over.

She began to walk, feeling his eyes on her,

feeling the silk flowing smoothly around her taut body—absurdly like a caress—annoying her that she should only now be so aware of the way cool silk felt against warm skin.

Trying for poise, a thing she never had to do these days because it had latterly become an extension of her personality, she asked as he fell in step beside her, 'What is it you want to know?'

The *Compton Gazette*, an evening paper with a massive circulation in the border counties, must be short on news if its managing editor, no less, had to come out here, offering to do a feature on her, she thought, her mouth curving slightly.

'I hadn't imagined my work was newsworthy, Mr Clent.'

He dipped his head to her, a smile for the wryness of her remark tugging at his mouth as his eyes flickered with warm assessment over the delicate purity of her features.

'It isn't, not yet,' he told her, his voice holding an enigmatic quality that brought her own eyes winging up to his, her sable eyebrows very slightly raised. But, mentally dismissing the question that quivered on the soft curve of her lips, she walked quickly ahead along the narrow gravel path that led to the studio.

It was cooler inside, light and airy, uncluttered and peaceful, the only piece of work on display the portrait of Bruno, a golden labrador, set against a background of autumnal moors. It was finished, and all she had to do was cut it from the board, mount it and have it framed.

Lucas Clent made straight for the easel, his footsteps sounding loud on the bare pine boards. Intrusive.

People had come here before to what had been

Oliver's studio and now was unmistakably her own. Not many, of course, just the few who had somehow or other got to hear of her and her work, those who wanted to commission a watercolour portrait of a loved one—human or animal. Once it had been a house on the Welsh coast, a holiday home, squat and defiant at the head of an isolated cove. Tiah had enjoyed that commission more than most because she had stayed there on her own, while painting, and she had been able to find the tranquillity of mind she had, at that time, thought she had lost for ever.

And none of the people who had called here before had seemed intrusive, because their personalities hadn't had the power to touch her. They had remained as shadows, briefly acknowledged and then forgotten, drifting unfelt over the smooth surface of her life.

But Lucas Clent intruded. She didn't quite know why. He was a man, and he was certainly an attractive one. But she had had some dealings with men, from time to time since Oliver's death, and some of them must have been attractive, for pity's sake! It had to be more than that, something very much deeper, because no one had ever impelled her mind to transmit the warning messages that were growing louder and clearer by the second.

'I'm not wearing my newshound's hat this afternoon.'

His voice had a quality of warmth that had her defensively turning coolly away. Without even trying he was putting the stamp of his personality on her space. It was as unprecedented as it was intolerable. And the feeling that it should be so was quite ridiculous, and her consequent impoliteness demeaning in her view of herself.

Tiah made a very conscious effort to take herself in hand and moved over to the formica-covered counter, her body tall and straight, unknowingly graceful, like a shaft of moving light in her pale silk.

'Can I offer you a drink, Mr Clent?' Long cool fingers rested lightly on the top of the small fridge where she kept a supply of milk and fruit juices, her face half turned to him, her profile clear and classical against the paleness of the swinging curtain of her hair. 'Tea or coffee? Or something cold— orange juice? Lime?'

'Nothing, thank you.'

Those blue eyes held hers just for a moment and there seemed to be a question in the vivid depths, but if there was he didn't voice it, turning instead to the watercolour.

He has a clever face, she thought, and eyes that took in more than he admitted, eyes that wouldn't easily be fooled, and she caught herself frowning, knowing that she hadn't made such an involuntary assessment of anyone's character since Oliver's death.

'Do you have any more work you can show me?' Lucas asked mildly, breaking a silence he hadn't seemed to find uncomfortable but she had.

'As you see——' she gestured, deliberately vague, to the empty white walls which had once been covered with Oliver's canvases. She had more paintings, made for her own pleasure rather than commissioned, but she wasn't going to tell him so. They were private, and she was a private person, and she didn't know what his interest was in any case.

'Not to worry.' He had turned and those incredibly blue eyes were smiling at her again, holding a sexual challenge that made her catch her breath, and she veiled her own eyes quickly, hiding behind thickly sweeping sable lashes because hè might read the flicker of sudden sharp fear that must lie in her glance.

'I think I'd better explain what all this is about,' he added gently, as if her disquiet was something he could see and feel, as if he wanted to reassure. 'You've heard of the Guildhall in Compton?' He had moved to one of the tall windows, was looking out, so he couldn't see the nod which was all she was able to manage, the quick frown of her impatience. She didn't now want to know why he was here, she just wanted him out so that she could resume the quiet serenity of her disrupted day. But it appeared that he was bent on telling her, anyway, and she tightened her mouth with exasperation as he went on, 'Well, as you probably know, it's a fine medieval stone building, and two years before I was born my father rescued it. The council had plans for its demolition, so he bought it from them, had it restored and donated it back to the town as a gallery—a showplace for local artists, if you like, within the boundaries of the *Gazette's* circulation area. He funded it right through his life and did quite a lot of talent-spotting himself. And on his death I inherited his interest in the gallery along with the *Gazette*, and I'm here to ask you if you'd like to mount an exhibition of your work—some time this autumn, say? We can work out the timing details at a later date.'

She hadn't interrupted him, allowing him his say, because the sooner he'd finished the sooner he'd be gone. But she hadn't expected this, and a thread of uncontainable excitement brought sudden heat to stain her high-slanting cheekbones. Did he consider her work, on the flimsy evidence of the watercolour portrait of Mrs Planter's old labrador, good enough to allocate her space for exhibition? It didn't seem credible.

Oliver had once told her that her paintings were sweet, and she supposed they might be, in a simple, untutored way. She certainly could never have emulated the stark power of Oliver's style, and hadn't even tried.

'You can't be serious,' she said, shrugging, as her eyes were unwillingly drawn to his again. 'You've seen one——'

'Oh, more than one.' His wry grin told her he wasn't that much of a fool. 'So far I've come across "Plas Gwyn", Fiona Wycroft's little daughter Louise, and Midge and Ralph Bennion's Siamese cats.' He turned to study the work on the easel, his stance completely relaxed. 'I was having dinner with the Beresfords one evening about a month ago and they showed me your painting of their holiday home, "Plas Gwyn". Rightly, they were very proud of it and quite happy to tell me the little they knew of the artist—where you lived, your name, it didn't boil down to much more. But with their help I tracked down the other two paintings and was impressed by what I saw. You have real talent, Mrs Paradine; I'd like to help you get it more widely known—that's what the gallery's for.'

She felt his smile on her like a lover's touch, and it shocked her because she had been watching the way his mouth moved when he spoke, had noted the play of light and shade on his features, underlining his male attractiveness. Mentally, she backed off, pulling away from his persuasively dominant aura that seemed, against her wishes, to be reaching out and surrounding her.

'I don't think I want to be more widely known, as you put it. I'm perfectly happy as I am.' The words were politely dismissive, the way she deliberately walked to the door a rejection. Her body felt stiff, as if it no longer belonged to her. 'But thank you for coming out here, for taking the trouble.'

The smile she put in his direction as she offered that small sop to the conventions of polite behaviour was unconsciously and patronisingly gracious, and she would have cringed if she could have seen it for herself. As it was, she registered the straightening of his mouth, the lines of determination that clefted his lean cheeks, deepening in direct proportion to her cool dismissal of both him and his offer.

'You asked me if I was serious.' His tone was cool enough to take her breath away. Cool and smooth as steel. 'I don't make an offer like that unless I am. Largely due to my father's hard work, the gallery has a certain reputation to live up to.'

Unsmilingly, he took a card from an inner pocket, the pasteboard very white against the tanned strength of his long fingers. 'Phone me when you've decided to cut the condescending act and can let me know how long it will take to get enough work together to mount a decent exhibition.'

And that was that. Just that, nothing more. She watched him walk away and should have felt ashamed of her behaviour, but didn't. And the wave of relief that spread through her as he disappeared from sight was shattering in itself because she didn't even want that. She didn't want to have to feel anything. Even so, she felt reduced, as if he had taken something of her with him.

Turning quickly, shutting the studio door, she tossed his card on to a shelf, not looking at it, and began to cut Bruno's portrait from the board.

The shadows were lengthening when Tiah left the studio and made her way to the back of the house, letting herself in by the kitchen door. Polly was there, every fabric daisy on her blue felt hat quivering with silent fury as she prodded the steaming contents of an earthenware crock with a long-handled fork.

Tiah had never seen Polly without a hat. She decorated them herself to suit the season, her mood of the moment, and though many of her creations might look incongruous with her invariable uniform of a faded, patterned sleeveless overall worn over a drab cotton dress, Tiah knew the elderly woman would look more incongruous still, in the eyes of those who knew her, if she were ever to appear bareheaded.

'She's been in one of her funny moods again,' Polly pronounced crossly, banging the lid back on the crock and putting it in the Aga oven, slamming the door. She straightened up, her face flushed with heat and vexation as she held Tiah with bright black eyes. And Tiah smiled, her features warming with affection as the edginess that hadn't left her since Lucas Clent's visit began to recede. Thank the Lord for the blessed normality of Polly, she thought, asking, 'Shall I make a cup of tea, Pol? You've got time before you go?' knowing that Polly's troubles, large or small, could be soothed by a good strong cuppa. She slid the kettle on to the hotplate as the other woman eased her short stout person on to a Windsor chair at the head of the scrubbed pine table.

'I could murder a cup,' she confessed with a sigh that seemed to come up from her large black lace-up shoes, adding darkly, 'she's been playing that dratted music again, she'll end up in the loony-bin the way she's going, you mark my words. I thought she'd got over that daftness.'

In spite of the cheerful normality of the homely kitchen, Tiah shuddered. Fears that had been set aside for months now surfaced evilly again, because even worse than the whispering was the playing of the piece of music that had been Oliver's favourite——

'I know.' Tiah felt the skin on her face tighten and wondered if she looked as old and drawn as she felt as she poured two cups of tea and carried them over to sit at the table with Polly. 'I had hoped it was over and forgotten, too.'

But Claudia had been in an odd uneasy mood all day, infecting Tiah until she had been driven out of the house at teatime, her edginess compounded when the somehow disruptive presence of Lucas Clent had intruded into the solitude of Deepdene. It was almost as if Claudia had known he would come, bringing the havoc of the outside into the quiet seclusion of the tiny withdrawn world of two lonely bereaved women. But that idea was absurd, dangerously fanciful, and Tiah didn't know where it had come from. Her streak of common sense made her reject it out of hand and she told Polly, consciously soothing, 'Let's hope it's only a temporary lapse.'

'It had better be. Enough's enough. It's been over a year now and if anyone had the right to go bonkers it was you. But I've said it before, and I'll say it again—you've got a whole load more strength than anyone else I know, and you know how to

hide what you're feeling. And if she doesn't pull
herself together, smartish, she's in for the sharp
edge of my tongue!'

Polly sipped the scalding tea, her little eyes
snapping, and Tiah knew the anger was born of
frightened concern. Polly had worked at Deepdene
since before Claudia was born and her loyalty ran
deep. In her eyes, Claudia Paradine, the last
surviving member of the family that had taken a
raw, semi-literate country girl in, giving her well
paid employment for almost fifty years, could do
no wrong except when grief over the sudden, cruel
death of her gifted younger brother led to these
worrying manifestations.

'Something smells good!'

As if their troubled thoughts had conjured her
up, Claudia appeared in the open doorway, her tall
black-clad figure seeming to merge into the shadowy
passageway behind her, only the pallor of her face,
the whiteness of the smooth chignoned hair that
had not shown so much as a strand of grey before
Oliver's death, conveying the substantiality of living
matter.

'It's a casserole. Chicken and mushroom, and
Tiah made it before I got here this morning,' Polly
said grumpily, swallowing the remains of her tea
and reaching for her handbag. 'All I had to do was
put it in the oven at four, as per instructions, so
praising it won't soft-soap me! Any road,' she
heaved herself to her feet and straightened her hat,
'I'm off. And Joe won't be in tomorrow until gone
twelve because he's going with me to look over a
cottage that's come up for rent.'

'Oh?' Claudia came further into the room. 'That's
nice. Where is it?'

'Pear Tree Cottage—on Muncer's land. You

know it—old Mr Higgs used to live there.' Polly thrust her arms into her saggy grey cardigan. 'Muncer tried to sell it, but it all fell through, so it's up for rent again. Can't wait to get a place of my own and a bit of peace and quiet for once.'

Shortly after Polly's husband had died her son Joe had married, bringing his new wife to the tiny house on the edge of the village of Kinstan Lacy where Polly had lived since her own marriage. Joe was now the father of two boisterous sons, and another child was on the way and Polly yearned for a little peace and quiet. Tiah smiled sympathetically; poor Polly didn't get on well with her daughter-in-law and often said she could no longer call her home her own—especially as Joe, a jobbing handyman by trade, had converted the house to his wife's specifications.

'I'll keep my fingers crossed for you,' Tiah said and Claudia added, as if guessing that the blame for Polly's ill-humour could be laid at her feet,

'Tell Joe not to worry if he can't make it tomorrow; helping you has got to come first. It won't be the end of the world if the lawns don't get cut this weekend.'

And that was one big concession, Tiah thought as Polly marched out without a word. Claudia insisted that Deepdene was kept in a state of perfection, inside and out, and on the rare occasions that Joe had missed to come and cut lawns and rake gravel there had been hell to pay.

'Have some tea? There's plenty in the pot.' Tiah had been watching Claudia, practically holding her breath. But she had seen nothing to hint at the mental disturbance that had shown itself earlier today, and her tense muscles relaxed as relief trickled through her. 'And the casserole's ready when you are.'

'Let's have a Martini first—nice and dry. Forget the tea.' Claudia's slow smile was endearing, making her suddenly look younger, and Tiah nodded as her sister-in-law moved to the door, saying, 'I'll go and pour the drinks and we can eat later. And by the way——' she paused in the doorway, poised, serene, 'you must allow Polly to prepare the meals. That's what she's paid for.'

'She's no spring chicken,' Tiah smiled thinly, carried the used cups over to the sink, then fetched the greens she had washed earlier that day from the fridge. 'Besides, I like helping around the house. It gives me something to do.'

'Maybe. But Oliver wouldn't have liked to see you turning into a drudge, and you have your own hobby to keep you busy. If Polly can't manage on her own, bless her, we'll employ someone to help. It's not your place.'

As the older woman drifted away to fix the drinks Tiah shook her head, wrinkling her nose. Claudia was a dear and her only real fault was her inborn snobbishness—and even that had its amusing side sometimes. Fond as Claudia was of Polly, she was a hired servant and there was a line between employer and employee which could never be crossed.

'This is nice.' A pile of fir-cones burned in the Adam fireplace and the flickering light of the flames softened the gauntness of Claudia's features, making her look ageless, and Tiah agreed that yes, it was, and wondered why she was lying.

Normally, she enjoyed the tranquillity of the quiet evenings they spent together, Claudia's long pale hands busy with her embroidery, not hurried but working with the air of inexorability that was so perfectly in tune with her character. Tiah herself was usually content to bury her nose in a book, only half alert to her surroundings. But tonight she was plagued with a vague sense of restlessness she couldn't begin to explain away.

Oliver seemed very close. His paintings hung on the walls, covering them, so that very little of the soft sage green wall colour could be seen, and his face smiled at her from a silver frame on the little rosewood table at the side of the hearth and regarded her quizzically from an identical frame on the mantelpiece. And if she turned her head she would see him again—with a fishing rod in one hand and a three-pound lake trout in the other.

All the photographs of Oliver, and there were dozens of them around the house, had been taken before Tiah had known him and went back to his christening. Claudia had produced them soon after his death and Tiah had known that they had been brought out as a gesture of comfort—'See,' she had almost been able to hear the thought in Claudia's mind, 'he is still with you, still loving you.'

And at the same time she hadn't had the heart or the energy to tell her sister-in-law that seeing her lost husband's face wherever she looked had pained her beyond belief, or to object when Claudia had asked Joe to carry Oliver's canvases in from his studio and hang them around the house. Claudia had only been doing what she thought best—it had been her way of offering comfort to the grieving young widow. She had been trying to ease a sorrow that could never be eased, to keep Oliver close in the only way she knew how.

And later on, when Tiah had managed to find herself again, to come to terms with the future, it hadn't seemed to matter.

She put her book aside, unable to concentrate, and crossed the Persian carpet, her feet making no sound in a room which was silent except for the crackle of the fir-cones.

'Would you like a drink?' she offered, and when Claudia smiled and shook· her head she poured a Scotch for herself and without quite knowing why, said, 'I had a visitor this afternoon. A Mr Clent.' She hadn't meant to mention his name, or his visit, and couldn't imagine why she had, except that the wretched man seemed to have carved himself a place in her mind, his presence there an irritant. And somehow it helped to hear his name on her lips. Relieved the pressure.

'Do I know him?' Claudia's hands smoothed the fabric she was working on, moving with near reverent care over the fine design, her head tilted just slightly.

'I shouldn't think so. He's the owner and managing editor of the *Gazette*.'

'Not *Lucas* Clent?'

Alert, as she had been all day for signs of distress from Claudia, Tiah picked that one up, but the sudden stillness of the long pale hands, the perceptible stiffening of the narrow shoulders, could have nothing to do with her tacit grief for Oliver, grief that was eating her up inside because she had never once openly admitted it.

'That's the one.' Tiah spoke casually, her tone throwaway, her movements perfectly relaxed as she resumed her seat on the opposite side of the hearth to Claudia. But it had been an effort; she was far from relaxed inside because every particle of her being was alert, tuned in to the vibrations that man had left behind him. They inhabited her space. She did *not* want this feeling of suddenly being aware again, her cosy limbo had suited her fine, but she didn't know what she could do about it, except try to ignore it, and she wasn't doing well in that direction.

'What do you know of him?' she asked.

'Nothing good. What did he want?'

'He asked if I'd like to mount an exhibition at the gallery in the old Guildhall.' Tiah ran a finger round the rim of her glass, not looking at Claudia but perfectly aware of her dark, narrow gaze.

'An exhibition? *Your* paintings?'

There was disbelief in the older woman's tone and something more. Bitterness? But Tiah couldn't credit that, she was strung up enough to imagine anything tonight. Claudia had been surprised, but pleased, too, when Tiah had received her first commission, and they both knew that Tiah's work couldn't be called art—unlike Oliver's. So Claudia might be surprised that Tiah had been offered space for an exhibition, but bitter? Never!

'That's what the man said.'

'And what did you say?' Claudia wanted to know. 'You told him you wouldn't have anything to do with it, I hope?'

The question was harshly put and its urgency took Tiah by surprise, but she answered reassuringly enough because she didn't want to upset Claudia by asking why Lucas Clent was bad news as far as she was concerned—not after today's regression, she didn't.

'Words to that effect, yes.'

'I'm glad. It would be foolish to lay yourself open to ridicule. And now I think I'll change my mind,' the soft smile was contrite, 'and ask you to give me just the tiniest drop of brandy.'

Tiah got to her feet at once. She didn't think there was any danger of her work being ridiculed. Ignored, maybe, but hardly mocked, and she couldn't imagine why Claudia feared it could be. But she knew Claudia hadn't meant to be unkind, she would never hurt anyone, not knowingly, especially not Tiah on whom she tended to lavish all the devotion she had once unstintingly given to Oliver.

There was a dog barking somewhere, on one of the farms. The sound was distant, but strangely magnified on the still night air. The deep blue curtains moved only slightly at the open window, and Tiah, leaning against the sill, felt the soft slide of the cool air against the bare skin of her arms and she shivered, although the night was far from cold.

To anyone standing out there, looking up, she would appear wraithlike in her white nightdress, her long pale hair covering her shoulders. The thought amused her, and she smiled. There was no one out there, looking up, they were far too isolated for that, and the only thing that moved down there in the night was the stream as it murmured sleepily to itself on its stony bed. She enjoyed the sound, it relaxed her, helped her to drift to sleep in her little blue virginal room.

She had moved in here on the night Oliver had died, unable to face sleeping alone in the great mahogany bed with the inlaid swags of roses where they had lain together for, literally, six hundred nights. And her nights had been peaceful in her little blue room except for sometimes, when the dreams came. And that wasn't too often, not now, thank heavens. But tonight she knew that the sound of the stream below her window wouldn't work its customary magic.

And as she left the window and slid beneath the pale blue counterpane she cursed Lucas Clent, who had come with his intelligent blue eyes, his aura of velvet-gloved domination, the unmistakable sexual challenge she had picked up from his every movement, his every look, frightening her by the effortless way he had placed the stamp of his personality on her mind, reminding her of things she had imagined forgotten. He made her feel like a small animal, caged for so long that the scent of freedom had slid a long way back beyond consciousness, only to be given, just for a glimmer of time, a sharp recollection of how it once had been. A recollection brought about by a passing stranger who had never been a stranger at all.

Her thoughts grew jumbled, grumbling away in her tired mind, and she was brought back at last, from the tentative edge of sleep, by a vision that was clear enough to be seen, etched vividly on the inside of her eyelids, of the way Oliver's eyes had possessed hers when she had cradled him in her arms as he'd died. And the last words he had ever said, every slight variation of intonation, crystal clear in her mind——

'Don't grieve for me, my Tiah. Never grieve. I'll never leave you. Wherever you are, wherever you go, I'll be there with you. Loving you.'

CHAPTER TWO

COMPTON High Street wore its Saturday morning face; the sedate, mostly Georgian buildings, the sober shop windows, engulfed in the colourful raucous tide of the street market. Traders bellowed improbable praises of their wares and customers jostled, intent on snatching the vaunted bargains from the piles of produce, the gaudy cheap-and-cheerful fashions that fluttered enticingly in the soft May breeze.

Tiah enjoyed the sense of chaos, the pushing, perspiring throng of humanity, the colour, scent and noise. There was life here, there was good-tempered confusion, and it flowed around her but did not touch her because she had learned to hold herself apart. The good-humoured crowds were little more than moving shadows—lively, of course, but still shadows. Actors in a moving set piece, reinforcing the reality of her own isolation. Shadows, actors, whatever, they made no demands, asked nothing of her, and that was how she liked it.

She had left the portrait of Bruno at her usual picture framers and had matched some silks for Claudia who had declined Tiah's invitation to drive into Compton with her. Claudia, thank the lord, had seemed quite rational and normal this morning, so Tiah had had only the smallest of qualms over leaving her on her own.

Tiah drifted with the crowd, her mind idling. The

sun was warm on her back, striking through the lightweight linen suit she wore—severely yet elegantly cut, its colour matching the silvery grey of her eyes. Then all at once the street was quieter, the broad pavement empty except for a woman with a pushchair and she realised, with a twinge of real annoyance, that without her being aware of it her feet had deposited her outside the old Guildhall.

Gilt letters on a black sign burned into her brain: 'The Gallery', and she was sick with herself for turning up here. Although she had banished Lucas Clent's invitation from the forefront of her mind, it had obviously lodged itself in her subconscious. But while she was here she might as well take a look around and hopefully rid herself of the devil that was the disquieting presence of him. She thought she had shifted it, but obviously hadn't.

One of the ground-floor rooms was a coffee shop, so she would treat herself to a cup after she had viewed whatever there was to see. She glanced at the printed billboard. The current exhibitors were a local sculptor and a jeweller from just over the Welsh border.

The gallery was silent, like a museum, and sunlight washed peacefully in through long mullioned windows. She had the place to herself and was impressed by the quality, the strength of the sculpted figures and she remarked on the unknown artist's obvious talent to the elderly caretaker who sat on a chair in an alcove between the two exhibition rooms.

'We only show the best.' he told her with vicarious pride, handing her a leaflet giving details of future exhibitions which he took from a neat pile on the card table at his side. 'We don't offer space for rubbish. And you'd be surprised how word gets around. Lots of serious collectors get here.'

'Is that so?' A few butterflies began to bump around in Tiah's stomach. She had been offered space for an exhibition of her own, but how could her work possibly be called 'the best'? Oliver, with the true artist's integrity, had called her work 'sweet', the faint praise damning in itself, and probably more than it deserved. 'Is it difficult for an unknown artist to mount an exhibition here?'

'Difficult!' Rheumy old eyes were raised expressively. 'There's a waiting list of hopefuls as long as your arm.'

'Yes, I suppose there must be.' Tiah folded the printed leaflet and pushed it inside her grey suede shoulder bag. 'How long has this place been functioning as a gallery?'

'Let's see now.' He scratched the back of his neck. 'Mr Clent senior, that was, bought it off the council thirty-nine—no, thirty-eight years ago, and it opened as a gallery a couple of years after that.'

So that makes Lucas Clent around thirty-six years old, Tiah thought, annoyed by the way he intruded on her thoughts. She wasn't interested in his age, or anything else about him, and she would have passed on, into the next room where the jewellery displays were, but the caretaker was chattering away, enjoying the chance to talk to someone, imparting information she didn't want to have but, short of downright rudeness, she couldn't evade.

'Yes, this place has earned itself quite a reputation. Old Mr Clent made it his hobby and in the end it took up so much of his time that he neglected the *Gazette*. When he died four years ago the circulation had dropped to next to nothing, but then young Mr Clent took over and things really got going. Installed a new plant, brought fresh blood in on the editorial side—really gingered things up, he did. Us here, at the gallery, thought we'd have to take a back seat, couldn't see him having the energy to spare, let alone the time to take an interest the way his father did—what with him dodging between here and the States. But not a bit of it.' He grinned suddenly, displaying a set of alarmingly white false teeth. 'If anything, he's even more particular than his father. A real go-getter, is Lucas Clent.'

'That's nice.' Tiah smiled distantly, evading a further flow of unwanted information with polite diplomacy. 'I think I've just enough time to look at the jewellery.'

Thankfully, the caretaker didn't follow her into the next room, and she stared at the glass-fronted showcases, not seeing the displays because she could only see, printed on her mind, the way the 'go-getter's' warm blue eyes had smiled into her own before she had turned them to chilling ice with her offhand dismissal of his offer.

If the caretaker was to be believed, and she saw no reason why he shouldn't be, then the work of aspiring new artists, those who were allowed to exhibit their work here, had to be of the highest quality. And Lucas Clent had taken the trouble to track her down, on the strength of seeing three examples of her work, and that had to be the most flattering thing that had ever happened to her.

Flattering, but hardly credible.

Lost in her thoughts, nothing else impinged, so she all but leapt out of her skin when the educated, deeply masculine voice came from right behind her.

'You've had second thoughts, Mrs Paradine?'

She would have known that voice anywhere. Its cultured, slightly husky quality was, unfortunately, grooved into her brain. Embarrassment coloured her face. She felt as though she had been discovered doing something shameful, and she kept her eyes firmly fixed on the showcase in front of her, not turning to face him because he was shrewd enough to be able to read the way she was feeling.

'Not at all. I just happened to be passing.'

The throwaway statement had all the hallmarks of a lie. No one 'just passed' the gallery because the street led nowhere except to a couple of furniture warehouses and, further down, the abattoir. But the words had been enunciated coolly enough, and she had herself and her colour back under control again, so she turned, prepared for, yet still unnervingly affected by, the impact of those incredibly blue eyes, that strikingly attractive face.

He looked as though she were the only thing that interested him at this moment, his undeniable charm, his time, entirely at her disposal. And that alarmed her.

Prickles of warning apprehension crawled up and down her spine, as they had yesterday, and she felt gauche, desperately so, but didn't have time to wonder at her reaction because he asked, oh-so-lightly, 'If you've seen all you wanted to see, shall we have coffee downstairs? Take a first step into friendship?'

'Is that necessary?'

'Which? The coffee or the friendship?' One dark straight eyebrow moved quizzically upwards and that, more than anything else, rankled with her because she had never been able to master that small but telling expression of superiority. And she couldn't think what had come over her. Normally she would have had the panache to say sorry, she was pressed for time, or some such—not fling out a stark question that sounded like a challenge.

The last thing she wanted to do was challenge him

on any level. She wasn't sure she was up to his weight. But he took matters out of her hands, his fingers tightening on her arm as he gentled her towards the doorway, with a passing and pleasant remark for the caretaker, his voice low when he turned to her again, his warm clean breath brushing the side of her face.

'Both are necessary. But perhaps not wise, Mrs Paradine?'

And whatever he meant by that enigmatic remark she hadn't the wits to fathom because whatever it was about him that had surrounded her, impressed itself on her yesterday, was doing so again.

Feeling trapped, imprisoned by him and by something within her that responded to him like the tide to the moon, she allowed him to escort her back down the stairs, seat her at a red-linen-covered table, order coffee from the hovering waitress.

'What did you think of the current exhibition?'

'Impressive.' Tiah's eyes were fixed on his strong finely made hands as he poured cream into his cup. And something, some wayward careless streak in her, made her ask, 'So why should you offer me space, Mr Clent? I wouldn't have thought my work came anywhere near the high standards you demand.'

The words had come spilling off her tongue, past the censor of her mind, which would have banned them because they invited further involvement and that, no matter how briefly, was something her most basic instincts had been warning her against since she had first set eyes on him.

'Now I wonder why you should think that.' His eyes were intent on her face, as if he had the ability to read her thoughts from the suddenly shuttered silver eyes, the slight frown between sable brows, the full wide mouth that quivered softly before being consciously firmed, offering no compromise.

She shrugged, her slim elegant shoulders lifting just slightly. No need to tell him that her work had been damned with faint praise from a man who had been a true artist, that Oliver, though loving her almost obsessively, had been unable to find any hint of real artistic integrity in her work. That if anyone could have found that sign of true talent, he would have done, because he had loved her.

Sipping her coffee, she declined to answer and was relieved when he seemed happy to leave the subject, but even so, she was exclusively aware of him. Everything else, the scarlet-clad tables, the other customers, the two waitresses in their pretty uniforms of Laura Ashley print, became part of a world that was blurred, out of focus, a shadowy backdrop against which only he was real, his presence, and the effect of it, overpowering.

She was strangely afraid of him, no doubt about it, afraid of the power he had to spark this awareness in her, afraid of the way her breathing seemed difficult to control, of the fine inner tremor that weakened her bones.

Lifting her troubled eyes she saw that he was leaning back in his chair, his gaze wandering with superficial idleness over her, from the pale ash-blonde hair which she had scooped back today, down the pure line of her slim young throat, to the deep V of the severely cut suit jacket where pale skin glistened between the long narrow lapels, and a pulse throbbed erratically as if waiting for his slow, soothing touch.

But there was nothing really superficial, or idle, about the journeyings of his eyes. He was taking stock in the deliberate way of a man whose interest has been caught and held and Tiah had never before been so conscious of the fact that she wore nothing beneath the lightweight jacket, and that he knew it. That her heart was pounding wildly beneath her breast—and that he knew that, too.

The coffee had been hot, there was more than half a cupful still left. She would drink it, say something innocuous: 'I do hope this fine weather lasts, don't you?' pretend an appointment—the hairdresser, perhaps, and go. She twisted the wide gold band of her wedding ring, and he asked, 'Was this your first visit to the gallery?'

Tiah grasped at the conversational straw. Anything to divert his mind from that slow, deliberate perusal.

'I'm afraid so. I don't come to Compton often. Claudia and I can get most things we need in Kinstan Lacey.'

'Claudia?'

The tilt of his well-groomed head, the lifting of one corner of his long, very male mouth, was an indication of the workings of his probing mind. She felt he was reaching for any scrap of information about her, filing it away in his head, and it troubled her because the more he knew of her, the more he would violate her inner tranquillity, the quietness she guarded so carefully because once it was shattered all manner of disrupting things would be free to enter.

But surely Claudia was safe territory? And a little idle conversation to fill these final taut moments was better than the strange, electrifying silence where thoughts tended to follow half-hidden tracks that were better left undisturbed.

'My sister-in-law. We find all we need quite locally. We don't stir ourselves to go further afield very often, I'm afraid.' She smiled self-deprecatingly, a self-condemnation that wasn't sincere because she was content with the situation. But the smile was wiped clean from her lips when he commented, almost scathingly,

'So you've hidden yourself away in your little lost valley, letting your sister-in-law keep the big bad world from your doorstep, ever since your husband died. Don't you think it's time you came out from behind Claudia's skirts and took just one step out into the unknown?'

Tiah's eyes winged up to his, wide and scared, the pupils deep black pools of fear. So he knew she was a widow, and the wedding-ring she still often wore was no defence against him.

But Oliver's death would have been reported in his paper, of course. There had been an inquest, photographers, questions. However, he mistook the reason for her fear, and that amused her a little, relaxed her, made her glad that he couldn't read her as well as he obviously thought he could. But the reassuring hand he placed over hers produced tremors of deep unease, coupled with a tingling sensation that grew, enlarging until it reached every last part of her.

'After the first step, Tiah, the next would be easier, and the next easier still. Don't you understand that? Don't you want to find yourself, come out from behind Claudia's sheltering skirts, as it were?'

There was a new soft depth of kindness in his eyes, the stamp of concern gentling the aggressive male attractiveness of his face. And it was all misplaced, and she felt sorry for that now, because his concern, his kindness, was real. But she assumed her habitual mask of serenity, withdrew her hand from beneath his and let it lie calmly with her other in her lap.

He had got it all wrong. She had chosen to stay with Claudia after Oliver's death because she had seen that she was needed. True, she had thought of leaving, finding work, a place of her own. She had even asked Polly if she would like to move in, live at Deepdene, because Claudia couldn't really be left on her own, whispering to the dead man, filling the house with his paintings, with photographs that went back to his early childhood, playing tapes of his favourite piece of music, but never once weeping, never admitting her grief, talking as though Oliver were still there. Unseen. Unheard. But still there.

Polly had categorically refused to move in, even though she disliked living with her son's family, her fondness for her employer taking second place to her dread of spending so much as one night in the house which a dead man still inhabited, unable to rest because Claudia refused to let him go.

So Tiah had stayed. Her gratitude to Claudia for having provided her so generously with a loving home background for the first time in her life made her unable to desert the older woman. That, and her own deep sense of guilt, had kept her at Deepdene, against her inclinations at first, until she had come to terms with it and had found her own brand of contentment, the inner security that made her realise that things were better this way.

However, she wasn't about to tell this man as much. The reasons for being at Deepdene, for isolating herself, were her own. Let him keep his opinions, no matter how wrong they were. Let him think her a cringing coward, unable to face life, if he must. It was nothing to her. She smiled politely, 'Thank you for the coffee, Mr Clent,' and gathered up her shoulder-bag.

'The name's Lucas.'

The quiet words halted her unhurried movements. She hadn't missed his own use of her Christian name. She inclined her head, giving nothing away, quite in control again, or so she thought, all the more shattered at the shooting excitement that surged through her as he told her, getting to his feet, waiting for her.

'Please think very seriously about working for an exhibition, Tiah. For some crazy reason you don't seem to have confidence in your work—but I do. You have very real talent and I'd like to see you extend yourself, take that first step I was talking about earlier. Promise me you'll think about it?'

Her eyes swept his face, searching for something, then slid away again as her heart began to thump beneath her ribs. Why not? *Why the hell not?*

It was a challenge, an exciting one, and although her clients had all expressed themselves delighted with her portraits of their children, pets, whatever, no one had ever come near to making her believe that her work held the seeds of real artistic talent. And it wouldn't necessarily mean that she need have anything more to do with the man who was now walking at her side, whose nearness had the unnerving ability to make her feet feel as though they were floating above the sun-warmed pavements. Quite the opposite, really, because once he knew she was willing to mount an exhibition he would stop hounding her, surely?

She stopped as they reached the intersection with the busy High Street, unwilling to endure his nerve-shredding company a moment longer.

'I'll think about it, Mr Clent. And I'll phone your office and let your secretary know, one way or the other, by Monday morning.' And then she turned, her long legs carrying her swiftly down the street.

And her heart was beating rapidly as she felt the undeniable tug of him, knowing it would take quite a concentrated effort of will to eradicate him from her mind.

The tight turn-off to Deepdene necessitated a careful slowdown and, once on the drive, Tiah braked, her hands resting lightly on the steering-wheel as she looked down at the house.

She had no idea what had made her stop to take such a long penetrating look. Deepdene was her home, and Claudia's, and even though she knew it was beautiful she hadn't bothered to take a real look at the house for a long time now. Always, except for a few fraught months, she had regarded the gracious house, sleeping in its quiet valley, as a place of love and refuge. A haven from the world outside. A place that for ever reached out and enfolded her comfortingly.

When Oliver had brought her here as his bride, and Claudia had made her feel so welcome and loved, it had become the home she had never had. And after she had come to terms with Oliver's death, and the pain of it, and Claudia's need of her, she had come to think of the house almost as an animate thing, a caring, consoling extension of the love Oliver had once given her.

But now, for some unknown reason, she recognised that Deepdene was not the warm enfolding place of her own wishful imaginings. It was nothing but a lonely house, a place apart, not welcoming at all but complete in itself, withdrawn, secretive.

Further down the drive, where wild hillside met tamed garden beyond the bridge and the glimmering curve of the stream, she saw Joe bend to start the mower, saw Claudia appear from the walled kitchen garden, carrying a trowel in her gloved hands.

The brief moment of insight pushed to the back of her mind, Tiah engaged first gear and the car moved forward and she was home again. And she determinedly dismissed the unpleasant feeling that nothing would ever be the same again because something outside the bounds of this lonely spot was making itself felt. Calling . . . calling . . . But she need not listen to that call, need she?

'I've been so worried about you.'

There was a pucker between Claudia's carefully darkened brows, and as Tiah straightened up after reaching for the packet of embroidery silks that had slipped between the two front seats she had to make a conscious and careful effort to hide an uncharacteristic sensation of annoyance.

'I'm not late for lunch, am I?' she tried for patience. She knew that, if she let her, Claudia would smother her with the possessive brand of love she had once poured out on poor dead Oliver. Tiah had known it, ever since that dreadful night when Oliver had died, known it and understood it, and had made sure that it had never been allowed to get out of hand.

'No——' Claudia's dark eyes widened, then she shook her head, turning away. 'Whenever you go to Compton you're *always* back in time for coffee. I was afraid you'd had an accident.'

'I had coffee there.' Tiah fell in step beside the older woman, pity softening her eyes, removing exasperation. Claudia had poured out all her love on the much younger brother she had brought up since they had both been orphaned. And she had lost him and was afraid of losing his substitute. It was something Tiah had learned to live with, largely by ignoring it, ostrich-fashion, and she was far too fond of her sister-in-law, too indebted to her, to assert her independence in any callous fashion.

'I see Joe turned up after all.' Tiah ignored the still, hurt expression on Claudia's face. 'So Polly must have made her mind up quite quickly about the cottage.'

'She's taking it.' Claudia walked through the open door at the side of the house, into the kitchen, stripping off her gardening gloves. 'Joe left her measuring up for curtains and carpets. She can move in just as soon as she likes.'

'I'm glad for her.' Tiah moved quickly round the sunny kitchen, putting the pizza she had made earlier that morning into the Aga oven, fetching salad things from the cool walk-in larder. 'She will be happier in a place of her own.'

'I doubt it. She's been used to having her family around her.' Claudia drifted to the door. 'Let's spoil ourselves, shall we, and have some wine with lunch? I'll fetch it from the cellar while you freshen up.' Her smile was warm forgiveness for the anxiety Tiah had caused. 'And just wait and see if I'm not right about Polly. She doesn't know what real loneliness is, not yet. And when she does she'll regret the move—noisy grandchildren or not.'

It was remarks such as that that dragged Tiah down. Waves of uncharacteristic depression hit her as she held a head of lettuce beneath the running cold tap. Claudia had a dread of loneliness. She was binding her tighter with her need, her dependence, her fear of being left on her own.

And Claudia's need was firmly cemented with Tiah's own sense of obligation. Her guilt. Although no one, not even Claudia, knew of that guilt. It was a burden she had to carry alone.

Not that she had any intention, now, of leaving Deepdene, of leaving Claudia alone. Their quiet way of life suited her, it made few demands on her, certainly none that could not be met with perfect equanimity. She had no desire to leave. Why should she have? So the sooner she got rid of the feeling of unease that had plagued her since Lucas Clent's coming, the better.

During what was left of the weekend she quietly contemplated the challenge of mounting her own exhibition, half aware that it didn't merit that much soul-searching because her mind had really been made up ever since Lucas Clent had expressed his opinion of her talent over coffee. But it was pleasant to have a choice, to feel she was in charge of her artistic destiny, either way. She could take the opportunity, or leave it. But she knew she would take it.

Instinctively, she knew Claudia would disapprove. But that was just too bad. Claudia didn't own her. And a simple thing like a showing of her watercolours wouldn't alter the affectionate, sisterly relationship they had.

Nevertheless, she would let Lucas Clent's secretary know her decision before telling Claudia. A cowardly attitude, she acknowledged, but she would be more confident, more able to deal with any objections, once she had formally committed herself.

So first thing on Monday morning she retrieved his business card from the shelf in her studio and dialled his office number from the telephone in the hall, overlooked by no less than four of Oliver's self-portraits. But the pleasant words she had ready for

Lucas Clent's secretary died in her mouth as he answered the call himself, and much as she would have liked to put the receiver smartly down and try again later she knew she couldn't be that cowardly.

He was only a man, after all. That he affected her in the way she had vowed no man would ever affect her again—not after Oliver—was something he would never know.

She found her tongue, found the words coming blessedly smoothly after his second and slightly puzzled, 'Who is that?'

'Tiah Paradine. Just confirming that I'd like to take the space you offered at the gallery.'

There was a small, taut silence, charged with the inexplicable something he so effortlessly produced from her—and something else, quite indefinable—from his end. And then his voice came, warm, pleased with her, the waves of his pleasure reaching out and engulfing her.

'Good girl! Excellent! I'll come over to arrange a mutually suitable date—see how you feel about trying for the autumn, say. Eight o'clock this evening?'

There was plenty she could have said, she realised later, too late. Excuses she could easily have manufactured. But weakly, she found she couldn't, and later, long after he had rung off, she was cursing herself for denying the instinct for self-preservation, cursing him for making her something she had never been—easily moulded to another's will.

CHAPTER THREE

TIAH heard the distinctive throb of the blue car's engine as it slowed down to take the turn-off from the road. Kneeling on the floor of her studio, her portfolio of work open in front of her, she felt the alarming, tingling rush of adrenalin, the quickened pulse of her blood. *He was here*.

Defensively, she stared at the charcoal sketch in her hand. Oliver. His self-portraits, of which there were many scattered about the house, showed something she could never relate to, but this drawing was a fairly accurate representation of him as he had been when they'd first been married.

It was one of her earlier efforts, and Claudia maintained that it was far and away the best thing she had ever done, that the artist's love of the subject had captured the true beauty of the man.

But beauty was in the eye of the beholder, and Claudia was biased.

If she looked long and hard at the drawing, absorbed his image into her mind, it would recall the time of her marriage, his ways of loving her. Remind her, deeply and explicitly, so that Lucas Clent's powerful male magnetism would lose all power to affect her, become something she could handle . . .

Her fingers shook as they trailed softly over the surface of the paper as if the sense of touch could reinforce the sense of sight, planting the image still more deeply—the softly tousled pale hair, the hooded, slow dark eyes. Eyes which had held something haunted and which, miraculously, she had been able to capture. The fine aquiline nose, the thin mouth curved into the smile she knew so well . . . Mocking . . . Knowing . . .

Sudden painful tears glittered in her eyes and she could not stop them, or still the trembling of her hands as she dropped the drawing back into the portfolio. Hearing the slam of the car door, the sound of his feet on the gravel, she almost ran to the door in her need to prevent him going to the house.

Claudia had been told of the exhibition and Claudia had not been pleased. Understatement. She had been acidly antagonistic to the idea. And heaven knew what she might say or do if Lucas Clent walked in on her now.

She blinked back the wretched tears as she called to him from the pathway, and although he didn't comment she knew her distress had registered with him as he strolled towards her. His eyes were keen and the arm he dropped around her shoulders as they walked together into the quiet studio was comforting, as no doubt he intended it to be. And she didn't want that.

Shrugging away from him she moved over to the counter, deliberately bright, everything on the surface.

'I'll make some coffee.' Plugging the kettle in, her movements brisk and unfussy. Outwardly cool but inwardly seething with feelings: fears, longings, all too complex to be given recognition.

'I thought we could talk things over more quietly here,' she remarked frigidly. 'You mentioned the autumn—early, or late?' She had reached cups and saucers from the cupboard. Pretty. Bluebells on a cream backround. Bluebells always reminded her of Oliver, of that first spring when the woods had been full of them, and without even trying she could smell the crushed stems and ruptured blossoms, strewn on the ground where they had lain . . .

The shaming tears glittered again and the lump in her throat rose to choke her and Lucas said quietly, from the other side of the room, 'So you do have more work' and she turned and saw that he had rested the portfolio on top of the bench and was looking at the portrait of Oliver.

'Ah—yes. Some of it's very early stuff.' But not all of it was early. Some she had done since Oliver's death, purely for her own satisfaction, and she swallowed hard, tried to smile to give lie to her wet eyes, her painfully husky voice, because her griefs were her own, and her thoughts and feelings private, and the dark place of sorrow, deep inside her, was not open to anyone, certainly not to Lucas Clent.

'You were looking through them when I arrived.'

That was a statement, and if he connected her only partially hidden distress with the portrait of Oliver which he was now regarding so intently, then bully for him!

'Your late husband.'

And that was a statement too, and she noted the very slight stress he laid on the word 'late' and nodded when he put the charcoal drawing down, indicating the portfolio, 'May I?'

'Help yourself.' She left him to it as she made the coffee. She took her time, her unhurried movements calming her, and she was back to normal again when she took their cups over, putting his down on the bench.

He was holding a painting she had made of the bridge a couple of months ago. A sunny day, green water reflecting the pale light of early spring. A pleasant rural scene. But he said, 'You've one or two quite remarkable things here.' He dipped his head, eyeing the bridge scene. 'You've caught the essence of nature in this quite perfectly. Charmingly rustic on the surface, the sort of thing everyone looks for and expects, but you're hinting strongly at the darker currents beneath the surface of rural life. The vehicle of the stream, the bridge, is a perfect one for expressing your insight.'

'Oh?' Had she done that? It sounded very high-flown, and all she had set out to do was make a picture of one of her favourite parts of Deepdene.

Her bewilderment must have shown because he grinned down at her, suddenly, sideways.

'And you probably did it quite instinctively—— which doesn't make it less valid. You're what I'd call a primitive artist,' and seeing the way her face fell, relating 'primitive' to splodgy brush strokes and raw primary colours, he laughed openly, knuckling her chin with a gentle fist, drawing an uninhibited answering smile from her. 'By primitive I mean you're not stylised in your approach. You paint things the way you actually see them, feel them, without being influenced in any way, without being formal or contrived.'

He turned his attention back to the portfolio and she drank her coffee, watching him. His hands, as he sifted through her work—placing some paintings on one pile, some on another—were deft and strong and sure Beautifully proportioned, too. And he was wearing a crisp white shirt that accentuated his naturally dark skin, the nearly black hair that grew crisply into his nape, the breadth and whipcord strength of his shoulders . . .

And he turned, as if he had felt her eyes on him, and the half-smile left his face, the long mobile mouth straightening, his features suddenly hard with unmistakable wanting.

The breath caught in her throat and her hands shook so much that the cup rattled on its saucer, sounding obscenely loud in the thick silence that hung so heavily around them, tangible enough to be felt. It was as if her whole life had been leading up to this moment—the recognition of a stranger who was not a stranger at all.

He moved forward, so smoothly, slowly, that she sensed his increasing closeness rather than saw him make the conscious movement—as though they were being drawn nearer, ever nearer, without either of them having to do a thing to make it happen.

He took the cup and saucer from her unsteady hands, putting it down on the bench, his eyes never leaving hers and she knew what he was silently asking, wanting, and she spun round, caught off guard by the thing inside her that leapt to shocking life to reach out to him. She must not let him even guess at that weakness.

But he caught her as she turned, his hand firmly on her shoulder, spinning her round to face him again, and she felt frail, bewildered, trapped by the raw primal need that ached between them.

Her whole body trembled, a battleground for conflicting needs. He had the power to make her tremble, the power to force her to an awareness of her own pitiful vulnerability where he was concerned. And that knowledge could not lie easily with her mind's deliberate and conscious resolve to steer well clear of any emotional involvements. She could not become involved again. Not after Oliver.

The hand that had caught her slackened its grip, moving soothingly now, his fingers firing the skin beneath the light cotton top she wore. And his other hand moved against the small of her back, drawing her closer so that she was pressed against him, breast to thigh, knowing the warmth, the hardness of his body against hers as she melted to its unspoken promise, her trembling flesh growing still and soft and pliant beneath his touch.

Gradually, oh-so-gradually, with the soft pace of a long, slowly indrawn breath, his dark head came down to rest against the pale silkiness of hers and she knew that if he kissed her now she would respond with all the wanton ardour of a passionate nature long denied love.

Her pulses quickened, throbbing, as she felt the hardening of his body against the softness of her belly and her breath was shallow and ragged as she thought: Why him? Why this man? Why should he be the only man to penetrate the barrier she had erected with such painstaking care a year ago?

He had nuzzled aside the veil of her hair, his lips on her neck, sparking wild longings, his hands moving, creating havoc where there had been none until his coming, and she felt herself moving against him, mindlessly, her breasts rising, tensing, thrusting invitingly against him and one of his hands moved to accept what she was so blatantly offering.

But as his fingers shaped her, and she heard the sudden harsh rasp of his breath, telling her that his control was rapidly leaving him, she tugged away, appalled, her eyes darkening with shock.

How could she have put Oliver from her mind so easily? How *could* she! She had even forgotten the silent vow she had made as her husband lay dying in her arms. The promise that part of her, the part that could be subjugated to a man's sexual will, the masculine domination of the female senses, would never be allowed to surface again, no matter how strongly her body craved it. And her wanton near-capitulation in this man's arms had been nothing but a cruel, heedless denial of the promise she had so fervently made.

She turned her back on him, her shoulders rigid, and the ache inside her corresponding to the hurt, she knew without being told, touched him too. There was something about this man that was attuned to something in her; she knew how he was feeling, the pattern of his thoughts as clear to her as her own . . . It repelled and drew her at the same time.

As she heard the ragged exhalation of his breath she braced herself for what was to come. Knew he would come to stand in front of her. And when he did, not too close, and took both her hands in both of his, she accepted that, too, because she had no other choice.

'I'm sorry, Tiah.' The blue of his eyes had darkened to deepest indigo, his face hard-boned, serious, his voice husky with the contrition that was eating into him. 'You were already upset—seeing the drawing you'd made of your late husband, I guess. I behaved crassly. Forgive me?'

The touch of his hands warmed her, the gentle pressure of his fingers speaking wordlessly to her. She liked the feel of his warm dry skin against hers and she dropped her head, her hair falling forwards hiding the flush that rode high on her slanting cheekbones, feeling the heat of newly awakened desire spread to every part of her.

She couldn't speak, couldn't answer his plea for forgiveness because of the tight band that constricted her chest, her throat, making her breath come shallow and rapid because she knew she was just as much to blame for what had happened as he.

'Tiah——' The pressure of his fingers increased just fractionally and her head came up, drawn by a will stronger than her own. Long silver eyes searched his and she felt the effort he was making to achieve the respite of neutrality. 'There's a lot we need to discuss. So let's get out of here—go find some uncommitted space, the pub in Kinstan, say. Have a drink or two, talk about your exhibition, get to know each other.'

The desire to accept that invitation was strong, so immediate. It surprised her, took her breath away. But, firm with herself, her curt rejection, the swift removal of her hands from his, was proportionately strong. And before she turned, fussing with the coffee-cups, carrying them over to the counter, she saw the long male mouth harden savagely, the uncompromising jut of the strong jawline.

'Tiah——' 'The controlled harshness of his voice was shocking in the quiet room, and, her back still to him, she held her breath, tensing, not wanting a fight, but not daring to allow further intimacy. Wanting nothing from him, yet everything.

'Tiah, I'm offering you friendship, respect. Just that. I'll be honest, because with you of all people I can't see myself ever being any less than that— and tell you that I hope friendship will develop into something much more. You intrigue me, bewitch me—knock me for six, if you like. But until you're ready for that something more to grow I'll treat you with kid gloves. I won't force the issue, and that's a promise.'

He dragged in a long harsh breath, as if facing something that held terror for him but which, being the man he was, he had to outface.

'Now it's up to you. Take it or leave it.'

Her thoughts flittered this way and that, beating at the confines of her skull. She was sure she could trust him, could trust him with her life, and if all he offered was friendship she could handle that. Just. If she were very, very careful. And astonishingly, she found she wanted his friendship with a need that actually hurt, and she didn't want to face the aftermath of an evening that had been so disturbing, not alone.

Unconsciously, her shoulders relaxed and the face she turned to him was bright, the shadows gone as her full wide mouth curved into a smile that was beautiful, real enough to set sparkles of light dancing in her eyes.

'That seems like a nice idea, Lucas.' His name, spoken aloud naturally, felt good on her tongue and she grinned suddenly, enjoying his pleasure in her acceptance, knowing that she was herself almost absurdly glad they had reached this oasis of understanding. 'I'll ring through and let Claudia know I'll be out.'

She picked up the extension receiver, conscious of his eyes on her, smiling eyes now as he leaned against the bench, relaxed. The phone in the house rang out a couple of times and Claudia picked it up and she sounded breathless. Tiah was thankful the other woman hadn't left the receiver off again because she hadn't much wanted to have to face her and tell her what she had to say, not after the way she had taken the news of the exhibition.

'I'd been wondering if you'd got rid of that Clent man yet.' Claudia sounded almost as acid as she had done earlier. 'I've made coffee. If you want some you'd better come over before it gets cold.' The tone implied martyrdom and Tiah swallowed a sigh.

'I'm going for a drink with Lucas,' she said gently. 'I won't be late,' and replaced the receiver before Claudia could find something nasty to say about that.

She didn't need to change, not for the village pub. The navy cotton jeans and lighter blue shirt she wore struck the right casual note.

'Ready?' He was waiting for her, his hand on the door jamb, as if he couldn't wait to get out of here, and as she joined him, all at once feeling absurdly shy, he indicated the larger of the two piles of her paintings. 'You can get those framed, ready for your showing. And if you can produce half a dozen more this summer you're going to have a very successful exhibition on your hands.'

And that helped, it eased the way she'd been feeling, the inexplicable shyness disappearing with shop talk, and she found herself chattering to him quite naturally as they drove to the village, telling him what she had learned of Deepdene's history because he had asked and seemed interested.

The Rose and Crown in Kinstan Lacey was unashamedly late Tudor, unashamedly untarted-up. They were lucky enough to get table under the lattice-paned window and Tiah sat on the cushioned window-seat while Lucas went to the bar to get their drinks, waiting for him, wondering at herself for being here at all because she hadn't been out with a man since Oliver's death. Hadn't wanted to, hadn't felt the lack of male companionship.

She smiled, the movement of her lips automatic as he brought their drinks over, putting them down on the table, and she moved, made room for him on the seat beside her, her body responding immediately, like wildfire, to the nearness of him.

He had offered friendship, promising he wouldn't force a way through to something deeper, and she hoped they could keep things that way, but had her doubts. How could their relationship remain on an even, platonic level when he had already admitted he wanted much more, when she had seen stark need in his eyes, her own body responding to him with a violence that had shaken her?

Quickly, to hide her thoughts, she reached for her dry Martini, cradling the glass in her hands, her eyes narrowed as she watched the tiny crystals of crushed ice in the liquid move slowly, forming new patterns. And that was like life. New patterns emerged from the old, formed and reformed until the original was impossible to recapture.

She was no longer the poised serene creature she had been a few days ago. He had walked into her life, quietly—no rockets or thunderbolts to warn her—and had changed it, for good or ill, and she would never be the same again.

As if picking up her train of thought he lifted his glass to her in a wordless salute, his eyes sending intimate messages her own absorbed and probably, she thought disgustedly, returned!

But the brief, intensely personal moment was over and Lucas talked about her exhibition, putting her at her ease. She was to be given space for the month of October and she would need to get her work *in situ*, suitably framed, with an accompanying typed list of prices for Len Hutchinson—the caretaker—by the morning of the last day of September.

And this was fine, it gave them something neutral to talk about, and he went on from that to tell her of his years in the States, lacing his narrative with a dry humour that often had her laughing helplessly. He spoke of his years as a reporter and his gradual involvement on the editorial side, and then his plunge into ownership when he had bought a small and failing arts magazine, had made it his baby, building up the sluggish circulation until it became the most widely subscribed-to magazine of its type in the States.

'And you gave it all up to come back here?' Liquid silver eyes questioned his and he smiled slightly, ruefully, his wide shoulders lifting in an expressive shrug,

'I didn't give it up. I've a highly competent managing editor running the show for me until I can get back there—some time towards the end of this year.'

'So you'll be pulling out of the the *Gazette?*'

'No way.' His grin mocked her, as if letting her know she wouldn't be rid of him that easily. 'Four years ago, when my father died, I didn't want to come back—I'd made my life, my friends, in New York. But I'd inherited the *Gazette* and knew it was in poor shape—how poor I didn't realise until I had the figures in my hands. So I set about pulling it together because I owed it to my father. And I guess I've grown fond of the place, my roots are here, after all. So I split my time roughly seventy/thirty, the seventy percent being spent over here.'

'Sounds good,' Tiah sipped her drink. She was honest enough to admit that she was 'glad he spent the majority of his time here, but didn't think that state of affairs was at all wise. There wasn't a thing she could do about it, however.

He was leaning back against the upholstered back-rest, one arm stretched out along it so that his hand was almost touching her shoulder. She was totally aware of that hand, of the small space that separated them. If he moved his fingers, just slightly, he would be touching her. Her heart fluttered nervously, a translation of her fear of the way he could make her react, and she was pathetically relieved when he broke the taut silence, thick with unspoken sexual tension, asking her to tell him something about herself.

There was little to tell about the part of her life she was willing to share with anyone, but the bald facts about her childhood broke that tension.

'I was a broken-home kid. Oh, nothing traumatic,' she smiled gently as she noted the quick darkening of his eyes. 'My parents split up before I was old enough to understand what was happening. By all accounts it was completely civilised.' She slanted him a long silver look, smiling to indicate that she didn't have any hang-ups on that score. But she caught the continuing sympathy of his look and shrugged, twisting the stem of her glass, fixing her eyes on the swirling contents. She didn't want sympathy. She didn't need it

'I was left with my father. He was a busy man— an accountant with a large firm of property people— and my mother went to Portugal, to friends. I never saw her, not even a photograph. She remarried, and the last I heard—it must have been about ten years ago—she'd divorced again. God knows what's happened to her since. She's never tried to get in touch. Sometimes I wish she would, but it doesn't give me sleepless nights. Father didn't remarry, but he did have a series of live-in housekeepers who, I see with hindsight, lasted as long as they suited him in bed. He died when I was eighteen.'

'And you?' Lucas put in softly. 'How did the constant change of surrogate mothers affect you?'

'It didn't.' Tiah had to smile at that. She had never had much to do with any of them, they hadn't been interested in her. 'I was sent away to boarding-school when I was seven and my holidays were spent with paid child-minders. I hardly ever went home. There never was a place I could call home.'

Not until Oliver brought me to Deepdene, she added mentally. And that part of her life was something she wasn't prepared to share with him. So she said lightly, as if only just realising how long they'd spent over drinks and conversation, 'We seem to be the last here.' A quick bright glance at the wall clock that showed five minutes to eleven. 'Just look at the time!'

They said very little during the short journey back to Deepdene. And, letting him know she wasn't about to invite him in for coffee or a nightcap, she turned in her seat, her hand already on the door as the car slid to a halt on the gravel.

'Thank you. I've enjoyed this evening. We must do it again some time.'

She hadn't meant that, of course. Or had she? She had really only wanted to make her precipitate departure seem less abrupt. But he took her up smoothly, completely in control as usual, her will putty to be moulded by his demands.

'Of course we must, I'll pick you up at seven on Friday evening. We'll have dinner in town. Till then, Tiah.'

She was too flustered by his aura of total command to be able to find the words to refuse, and wondered whether she wanted to, in any case. And she was thankful the interior darkness of the car hid her heated cheeks when he leaned over to kiss her as she gathered herself together to scramble out of the car. She had half expected him to kiss her. The fact that he might had been on her mind during the entire journey back, making her wonder how she would react if he did.

On the one hand she could justly accuse him of breaking his earlier promise, giving herself a valid reason for severing their newly formed relationship at a stroke. On the other—if she responded to him, and she had good reason to suspect that her wretched body would take over from her better judgment again—then heaven only knew where it could lead!

But his lips were a mere warm brushing of her cheek, a featherlike movement against her lips. Nothing, on the face of it, that she could possibly take exception to. The brotherly kiss wasn't an anticlimax, though, or even a relief. If anything, it heightened the tension, increased her awareness, because she sensed just what he was holding back.

She watched the tail lights of his car disappear with a feeling that was an uncomfortable amalgam of relief and frustration. Like a child attracted to fire, she wanted to see him again. But the adult in her knew he spelled danger.

Several slow deep breaths of the scented night air helped her to pull her mind back to a semblance of calmness. From where she stood she could see the stream, the black water silvered by moonlight, the arch of the stone bridge throwing a solid shadow, and she caught the scent of water, the sound of it, and smiled to herself, relaxing. Some things were permanent, never changing in a world which, during the last few days, seemed to be shifting, out of balance.

But there was really no reason at all why she should get uptight over Lucas Clent. She didn't have to see him again if she didn't want to. The lord knew, he was determined enough, he had been proving that ever since they'd met. But she could be determined, too. And all she need do, if she decided against the Friday night date, was phone him and tell him so. No hassle.

But there again, he had the gentleness of the truly strong. He had demonstrated that, too. And she had enjoyed this evening—after they had made that pact. So, if she didn't think about the way he'd sounded when he had told her, 'You intrigue me, bewitch me, knock me for six,' she should be able to cope. And he had been honest enough about that, and she could trust him to keep his promise, couldn't she? And if she didn't think of those words of his again, or about how it had felt to be in his arms, then she should be able to keep her hold on a friendship which was already important to her and enjoy another pleasant evening with him on Friday.

Slowly, almost reluctantly, she turned to go in. No lights showed so Claudia must have gone to bed. Early for her. Claudia was a night creature.

The front door opened with accustomed ease,

yet somehow she felt she was an intruder in the aching silence of the house. The large hall was dim, the floor patterned with moonlight and black shadows. A chill seemed to have crept up from the stream, seeped into the house.

Tiah shivered, hugging her arms around her body, her sensitised ear picking up the faint whispering of fabric beyond the slow hollow ticking of the brass-faced clock. And Claudia appeared at the curve on the stairs. A dark shape, darker than the pressing shadows that seemed grotesquely solid, her face a pale undistinguished oval beneath the white aureole of her loosened hair.

'Claudia—you frightened me half to death!' Tiah fought for calm, injecting a note of banter. But her hand went to her breast, feeling the heavy thunderous beat of her heart.

'Did I really?' Cold the voice. 'I thought I heard a car. I've been waiting for you to come back. Waiting for hours.'

'It's not so late, surely! Look, can I make you a hot drink? I'm having one.' Annoyed, Tiah swung away, towards the kitchen, anger stiffening her spine. She understood Claudia's fears and, because she was fond of her, could sympathise with her. But she was a grown woman, she was entitled to go out if she wanted. And Claudia had no right to try to make her feel guilty because for the first time in over a year, she had spent an evening away from home.

But Claudia's voice stopped her in her tracks. The venom was difficult to ignore.

'I hate to think what's come over you, Tiah. It makes me shudder. What will poor Oliver think— going out with a man? *That* man!'

Appalled, Tiah turned and met the wild dark

eyes, dread clutching at her with icy fingers as Claudia drifted down the stairs, nearer, nearer, her voice penetrating, overloud in the night-time stillness of the old house.

'And don't try to pretend to yourself that Oliver doesn't know what you've been doing. He does. He promised he'd never leave you. And he hasn't, bless him. It is *you* who are breaking faith!'

Tiah felt sick, and cold, so cold. Shaking, she turned to go to the kitchen. Claudia was even iller that she had thought, her mental balance desperately precarious. She had been there as Tiah had cradled the dying Oliver in her arms. Claudia had heard those last pathetic words of his and had never, ever forgotten them. Had built on them in her mind until they had become a total fact.

CHAPTER FOUR

'How's Claudia been this morning?' Tiah had been working in her studio since eating a solitary breakfast. Claudia hadn't been around and she hadn't felt like seeking her out after the reception she had given her last night. She could still feel the impact of those febrile black eyes and needed to be able to come to terms with the shock before seeing her sister-in-law, talking to her, trying to decide what was best to do.

'Seemed all right to me. Spent the morning dusting.'

Dusting the silver-framed photographs of Oliver, Tiah thought darkly, meeting Polly's eyes and knowing by the way they suddenly widened then slid away that she had hit the truth.

Polly transferred the lump of dough from the mixing bowl to a floured board, her little eyes worried now.

'She *seemed* okay. Was asking about my new cottage—interested, like. She even told me I could look through the stuff in the attic and see if there were any bits and pieces I could use in the cottage. I wanted to mention it to you, ask what you thought. This place belongs to you both, your husband left it that way. So it's your things, too, as she's inviting me to make free with.'

'Oh—please take whatever you can find a use

for.' It would seem a pity to spoil Polly's pleasure in her new home with worrying talk of Claudia's mental health, but Tiah had to talk it over with someone. She touched the vivid petals of a geranium on the sunny window-ledge, inhaling the spicy fragrance, thinking how uncomplicated life would be if one were a plant in a pot. Sighing, she turned back to Polly. This wasn't going to be easy. But Polly had accepted her unquestioningly, as part of the Paradine family, when she had come here as Oliver's wife, and since his death they had grown closer, drawn together in their mutual concern for Claudia.

'I'm worried sick about her.' Tiah sat at the table, watching Polly work. 'You remember I told you that Lucas Clent asked if I'd like to mount an exhibition at the gallery?'

Polly nodded and Tiah rushed on, spilling the words out because they had to be said, no matter how distasteful she found it.

'He was here yesterday evening, and we went for a drink. And when I got back Claudia went crazy. She was talking as though Oliver were still alive—as if I'd been cheating on him.'

Her fingers were twisting together in her lap, her face set. She felt disloyal, talking about poor Claudia like this, even to Polly who knew of her employer's state of mind, and worried about it, too. As long as they could pretend that there was nothing too much wrong, nothing to get really anxious about, then the placid tenor of their lives could go on. Talking like this was like bringing something shameful out into the open, recognising it, making it real.

'You went out with him, and she didn't like

that?' Polly nodded sagely. 'Have you considered it might have been an act?'

'It didn't look like an act to me,' Tiah shuddered, remembering. The mental image of how Claudia had been had left a violent imprint on her mind. 'She looked crazy. It worried me sick.'

'She meant it to. Ask yourself how she'd feel if you went and got married again. She'd be left on her own and she'd hate that. Lo..eliness is one of her pet bugbears. I reckon she's blackmailing you. "Don't so much as look at another man or I'll go off my rocker." That's what she's really telling you.'

'I hadn't thought of it that way.' Polly could be right, many people subjected their nearest and dearest to emotional blackmail.

'Then you should.' Polly thumped pastry, taking her worry out on the harmless lump of dough. 'How old are you? Twenty-two? That's no age, and it's only natural that you wouldn't want to stay a grieving widow for the rest of your days. Stands to reason.'

'I've no intention of marrying again,' Tiah said through stiff lips. 'She doesn't have to worry about that.'

'No?' Polly's eyes were shrewd. 'Time will tell. You had a lovely man, and he doted on you, and you lost him and that was sad. But life goes on. And as for Miss Claudia—well, you'll have to be ruthless.'

The marigolds, the green satin bow that decorated Polly's hat today, swung around in time to the movements of her thick red arms as she rolled pastry. Tiah blinked and bit on a smile.

'I suppose you're right. I shall have to be.' But ruthlessness wasn't in her nature and she wanted

Claudia, to whom she owed so much, to be at peace with herself, happy, and she wasn't at all sure that last night's dark pantomime had been a blackmailing act.

'Don't get me wrong,' Polly asserted heavily. 'I think the world of Miss Claudia, but she'll ruin your life if you let her. I've seen it coming. She's a lovely lady, generous and warm, but she's got her faults like the rest of us. Spoiling young Oliver was one of them. Ruined him, she did, in my opinion, right from the moment she took over after their Ma died. Stood to reason, in a way. She'd always been a quiet, deep one. Even as a little girl she used to think far more than she ever said. And it affected her badly when she lost her Pa just before Oliver was born, and then her Ma when Oliver was going on three. Mind you, I always said that the raising of the little lad was the saving of her sanity. Poured her heart and soul into that boy, she did.'

The eerily haunting sounds of Saint Saëns' *Danse Macabre* filled the house many times during the ensuing days. It had been Oliver's favourite piece and he had taped it many times, a dark place in his soul responding to the music.

Apart from the playing of the tapes, Claudia seemed quite normal. Quiet, thoughtful, but perfectly rational. But Tiah dreaded to think what might happen when she heard of the Friday date with Lucas.

On Thursday morning Tiah knew she would have to cancel. She did not want to be responsible for a repetition of Monday night's crazy behaviour.

Lucas wasn't in his office but his secretary took

the message: Mrs Paradine would be unable to meet him as arranged. Her sister-in-law was unwell.

And that wasn't a lie. Physically, Claudia was fit, but her mental condition was another story. Sitting, a book in her hands, across the hearth from Claudia as they drank a pre-dinner sherry, Tiah noted how the other woman's eyes flickered restlessly, falling on one of Oliver's paintings and then another, moving on to the framed photographs as if she were taking a mental inventory.

If Tiah had been feeling strangely miserable because of the cancelled date, then watching Claudia now, she was glad she had done it. It was going to take time for Claudia to recover from the shock of Oliver's tragic death, and a great deal of patience and understanding on her own part, Tiah knew. And if she was capable of feeling so miserable over a cancelled evening out with Lucas, then it was just as well she had done it. She had no intention of getting involved.

When she heard the spurt of gravel beneath tyres, heard the clunk of a car door, she knew it was Lucas and got quickly to her feet, dropping her book. She might have known he wouldn't be put off by any excuse.

Casting an an anxious look at Claudia, who didn't appear to have heard the car's arrival, Tiah hurried through the cool gloom of the hall, opening the door before he had time to press the bell. She stared into his handsome face, her stomach muscles contracting, leaving her feeling weak. His expression was bland, polite, giving exactly nothing away, but she could sense the coiled tension in him and feared its unleashing.

'I was sorry to hear your sister-in-law was unwell. Nothing serious, I hope?' He walked in, as if he had every right, and the scent of the bouquet of white roses he carried turned her stomach. 'For Claudia,' he explained, his smile tight.

'Why have you come here?' Tiah's forehead was furrowed, her mouth dry. Claudia would throw a fit if she knew he was here. She was too fond of her sister-in-law, had too much respect for her, to want anyone to see her in a state of unbalance.

'We had a date and it would take an earthquake to make me break it.' His eyes left the taut oval of her face, sweeping round the spacious hall. Oliver's self-portraits hung on the walls, the trophies he had won for swimming during his schooldays set out on a highly polished side table, a bunch of deep purple pansies and soft blue forget-me-nots in a shallow cut-glass bowl in front of them.

'Where is the invalid?' He swung back to Tiah, his voice like silk, his eyes shadowed and grim. 'In bed?'

Tiah's heart pattered. 'She's——' and Claudia was there, tall and dark and watchful, in the sitting-room doorway.

'I thought I heard voices.' Her eyes questioned them and Tiah, her stomach clenching, tried for lightness.

'Claudia—meet Lucas Clent. He just dropped by for a moment.'

The silence gripped. Tiah's hands clenched at her sides, wondering which way Claudia would jump. Damn Lucas for coming here!

But the older woman merely nodded briefly, the inclination of her head dismissive as she turned back into the sitting-room.

Lucas followed and Tiah's eyes bored resentfully into his back, sourly noting his poise, the way the fine expensive fabric of his suit jacket skimmed the breadth of his shoulders, the sleek narrowness of waistline and hips. And suddenly she hated him, his intrusion a blatant challenge to her hard-won equilibrium. She had coped until now and he made past efforts seem worthless, the future uncertain, and she felt a nameless core of violence inside her reach out and meet the violence she sensed in him.

Claudia had resumed her seat, staring into space, and Lucas laid the white roses in her hands. 'For you.'

Tiah held her breath, her feet rooted to the spot. It was like waiting for a bomb to explode.

'How kind.' Claudia's long thin fingers moved slowly over the white petals, her eyes fixed on Tiah who stood in the doorway, spasmodic shivers rippling over her skin beneath the oyster-silk blouse and skirt.

'Tiah, won't you give Mr Clent a drink?'

She could feel his eyes on her, piercing her, as she crossed to the drinks cupboard, her fingers shaking as she dumped a large amount of Scotch into a squat tumbler, the neck of the bottle rattling against the glass.

So far, so good. At least Claudia was behaving rationally, taking Lucas Clent and his wretched roses in her stride—which was more than Tiah knew herself to be doing. But who knew what might happen—what crazy things Claudia might say—if Lucas didn't leave soon?

He was sitting in the chair Tiah had vacated, making himself at ease, setting out to charm as he complimented Claudia on her home. And as Tiah handed him the glass their fingers touched and the impact was like a jolt of electricity, making her suck her breath in through her teeth.

She saw Claudia's eyes on her, cold, hostile,

assessing, and she turned quickly. 'I'll fetch a vase for those roses, excuse me.' And when she returned to the room, bringing a white porcelain vase filled with water, they were talking as though they had been friends for years, and Tiah took the roses Claudia held out to her, and their eyes met, and Claudia's were warm, placating, so the momentary flicker of hard knowingness earlier must have been imagined.

She placed the long-stemmed blooms in the water, slowly, spinning the chore out, not wanting to be drawn into the little charade that was being enacted behind her. Whatever game Claudia and Lucas were playing didn't tie in with the facts as she knew them.

Claudia had been rabid at the thought of her growing involvement with Lucas, accusing her of cheating on a husband who had been dead for over a year. And yet there she was, chatting pleasantly and even—Tiah could hardly believe her ears— inviting him to stay and eat!

And his pleased, easy acceptance didn't tie in with the hard angry man who had walked into the house half an hour ago, his inner violence something Tiah had been painfully aware of.

'Shall I see to it, or will you, dear?' Claudia asked and Tiah pasted a smile on her face, pushing the last bloom into the vase, turning, gathering that the meal he had been invited to share was the subject under discussion.

'I will. You stay and talk to Mr Clent.'

Alone in the kitchen she breathed a little easier. Perhaps everything would be all right after all. She had set one more place at the circular table in the small breakfast-room where she and Claudia took their meals and had put one more plate in the warming oven.

But she was still uneasy with the whole situation, on edge, and she thrust a pan of prepared cauliflower on to the hotplate, the water slopping over, sizzling angrily, sucking in her breath as she heard his voice.

'You'll scald yourself if you go on like that.'

He was standing in the open doorway, hands pushed into the pockets of his narrowly cut dark trousers, his stance aggressive, his eyes hard, like frozen sapphires.

Stretched nerves jangled and Tiah snapped, 'Leave me alone, damn you!' appalled by the easy way he provoked her to this rare violence, by his quick, tight reply.

'I don't think I could, even if I wanted to.'

He advanced, slowly, and her panic mounted, choking her, and her fingers sought and found the knife she had used to prod the lamb casserole, and he reached her, taking the weapon from her nerveless fingers, tossing it harmlessly on to the table.

'Friends don't point sharp knives at each other.'

'You threaten me.' Her voice was a husky croak. She was digusted with herself for reacting that way, ashamed of the way her eyes clung to his, searching, seeking something solid, something reassuring in the emotional turmoil that bit so deeply, sending her crazy.

'You want me as I want you. That's why you feel threatened. The one wouldn't exist without the other. Friends don't threaten.'

He stood close, but he wasn't touching her, and she couldn't move because if she did he might move too, and it wouldn't be away from her.

'Friends . . .' The tip of her tongue flickered over dry lips and his eyes fell to her mouth, the sooty lashes making dark crescents against his tanned skin.

'You seemed happy enough with friendship the last time we met,' he told her smoothly. 'And I was content to let that state of affairs ride for a while.' His tone hardened, his words dropping like stones against rock. 'But don't *ever* lie to me again. There's not a damn thing wrong with Claudia. Fit as a fiddle, she tells me.'

His strong hands grasped her upper arms and she flinched, seared by his words, his touch.

'So why lie to me? Why hide behind needs Claudia doesn't have? Couldn't you have told me the truth?' And he shook her, incensed by her silence, the passivity she used as a weapon, the only one she had when he was so close.

'Goddammit! You don't need to spell it out, do you!' His hands dropped abruptly, and he thrust them savagely, deep into his pockets, his eyes holding murder. 'I only need to look around this place to see what a shrine you've made of it!' His lips curled derisively. 'I don't need you to tell me you're still too much in love with his memory to let another man near you. And that's okay. Fine. Because given time, I'll change your mind. Make you understand you weren't buried with him.' His anger was tearing them both to shreds. 'But don't ever lie to me again!'

He turned, as if the sight of her disgusted him, and she watched him walk out of the kitchen, her eyes blank. No way could she be disloyal to Claudia, betray her by telling of her irrational behaviour on Monday night, her own worries

regarding her sister-in-law's state of mind—precari-
ously balanced on the edge of an abyss which Tiah
couldn't even bear to contemplate.

Let him believe what he liked. It was, in part,
the truth. And it was her fault Claudia was this
way. If Oliver were still alive, Claudia would still
be as normal as daylight.

She was drained by the time Lucas took his leave,
too empty to dredge up a protest when he said
silkily, to Claudia, his eyes on Tiah, 'Tiah and I
will be having dinner in Compton tomorrow
evening. Something we can't wriggle out of.'
Suddenly, his eyes stabbed her, but the aggression
didn't colour his voice as he made his thanks for a
pleasant evening, adding, 'I'll pick you up at seven,
Tiah. Be ready.'

And that was a command if she ever heard one,
she thought as the door banged as he let himself
out, and she reacted edgily to the whine in
Claudia's voice, 'How often are you going to see
that man?'

If she starts telling me that Oliver won't like it,
I'll scream, Tiah told herself, her inner voice
already screaming.

But both of them being hysterical wouldn't
achieve a thing. Not a damn thing. Collecting the
used dinner-plates, the empty wine-glasses, putting
them carefully on the trolley, collecting herself,
she said evenly, 'Claudia, try to see it for what it
is. My friendship with Lucas isn't going to alter a
thing, how could it? I have a right to a life of my
own, I have to say that. But do you think that I
could ever get too involved with him—or any man,
come to that—after Oliver?'

She sensed the sudden tautness in Claudia, the

tense watchfulness, but continued clearing the table. It might be easier to say nothing more, safer, but she had to bring this thing out in the open.

'You've been—upset, ever since you knew I was taking up his offer of space in the gallery. Can't you tell me why?' She turned, and seeing the open distress on the other woman's face, left what she was doing and went to put a comforting arm round Claudia's thin shoulders, feeling the fitful trembling that seemed to go bone deep.

'You told me you were afraid my work would be ridiculed,' she said gently, hating to see the woman who had been like a mother to her, who had accepted her, made her feel part of a loving family unit for the first time in her life, look like this.

'Now why should my paintings be ridiculed? I know my work comes nowhere near the standard of Oliver's, but I don't think people will actually laugh, or throw eggs, do you?'

'You'll learn through your own mistakes. That's if you're determined to go through with it?'

'I am.'

'Then you'll learn the hard way. I'm saying no more.'

She had no doubt that he would come. Be ready, he had said, and she had dithered about that. Nothing to stop her getting into her car and driving deeper into the hills, staying out until bedtime, until he got the message, gave up.

The arrangements for her exhibition had been made, there was no reason for them to meet again. But running from him would be cowardly, and that wasn't her way, and such an action on her part would make him justifiably angry. And his anger she could do without. And it wouldn't be the end of it, not by a long chalk, she knew him too well to believe that.

So she would be ready. And she would be pleasant, because she didn't want to be his enemy, and she would try to make him understand that, while she did enjoy his company, she wouldn't be coerced, manipulated, taken over.

The evening was still and warm, and she was sitting on the white painted bench-seat at the front of the house, waiting for him. Out of the house, away from Claudia's dark hurt eyes, not wanting him to have to go inside, to cast scathing eyes over Oliver's 'shrine'—one of Claudia's making, not hers, but she couldn't tell him that without going into details she had no intention of sharing with him.

She shivered, cold despite the warmth, crossing her arms over her body, running her hands over arms that had suddenly got goose-pimples. And she heard the sound of his car and collected up her soft-tan leather handbag, collected herself, smoothing down the skirts of her tawny shantung dress. She was as ready as she would ever be and was confident of coping, fairly reasonably, if he chose to re-introduce their argument of the night before.

But his good behaviour sat immaculately on him, like a well cut glove, and his anger might never have been. Even when they halted outside a Georgian mansion on the outskirts of Compton, a house that had been converted to luxury flats, and not the restaurant she had been expecting, she was too much at ease in his company to object.

'I thought we'd eat at my place,' he told her,

pocketing keys. 'I cook a mean steak. You won't object?'

'Should I?'

'I won't give you reason to.' Blue eyes held laughter and she could share the joke because he was obliquely referring to what she had said last night about being threatened, and she knew he was doing what he said he would do, biding his time. But sometimes tomorrow never came, so she allowed him to lead her into the spacious foyer, his fingers cool and firm and almost impersonal on the soft flesh of her arm.

He took a key from his pocket and unlocked the lift. It was one of six and took them straight into the vestibule of his flat. There were seven panelled doors leading off, two bedrooms, two bathrooms, kitchen, sitting-room and study, he told her, and she grinned, 'Quite a pad for a bachelor. Sure you haven't got a wife and six kids tucked away?'

'Take a look for yourself,' he invited, turning away. 'Feel free to satisfy your female curiosity while I fix the salad and open the wine.'

Annoyed with herself for letting such a leading question slip out, she poked her nose round doors until she found the sitting-room. This was as personal as she wanted to get. His choice of furnishings—traditional and antique—set against dove-grey walls where two extremely fine paintings hung, reinforced her belief in the unambiguity of his character. He was essentially straight, honest, knew what he wanted and unerringly chose it. Which brought her back to his conversation of the night before and she didn't want to think about that, dared not, if she were honest about it.

'How hungry are you?'

He had come into the room while she'd been

staring out of the window, over the smooth expanse of sweeping lawn punctuated by great stands of rhododendrons and solitary beech trees, and she turned, smiling at the sight of him with a tea-towel tied round his waist, the impression he gave of a tiger trying to look like a domesticated moggy. And that should have warned her, but it didn't.

'Moderate to ravenous.'

The aroma coming from the kitchen was more than enticing and he disappeared to return moments later with a steaming platter of steaks, grilled tomatoes and mushrooms, asparagus spears and baby new potatoes.

They ate at the table at the far end of the spacious room, the food as delicious as it looked, the wine excellent and free-flowing, the conversation easy, keeping to neutral areas.

It started off well, the ebb and flow of talk bringing a clearer understanding, revealing shared likes and dislikes, a few differences of opinion, but nothing important, adding spice. Shared laughter, the sharp awareness between them carefully battened down. But there, if one looked for it. Carefully, she didn't.

All fine and dandy until he lit the candles, disdaining the main lights. And then the flickering glow moulded his attractive features, making them memorable, something Tiah knew she would never be able to put completely from her mind. She could not take her eyes from him and he groaned, dropping back into his chair, his jaw clenched. 'Don't look at me like that.'

She could have asked 'Like what?' all innocence and affronted dignity. But she didn't. She knew all too well that the way she had been looking at him, her eyes devouring him, had given her away.

She shuddered, heat creeping over her skin, an aching need deep inside her that was a direct response to the look in his eyes that was raw emotion.

He left the table where the candles flickered, turning the brandy in the glasses to mellow, amber fire, went to stand in the body of the room, away from her, his voice deep, roughened with something that could have been pain as he ground out, 'It's no damn use, is it, Tiah? I'm having the devil's own job keeping my hands off you.'

Watching him with wide troubled eyes, she knew he was right. It was pointless pretending they could limit their relationship to simple friendship. He wanted so much more than she was ever prepared to give, and she should agree with what he had said, it wasn't any use, then ask him to take her home, tell him it would be better if they never saw each other again. It was what she wanted, wasn't it? The best thing that could happen, given the circumstances, wasn't it?

He wanted more than she was able to give because, after Oliver, she couldn't give to any other man. But he was hurting, torn by an anguish she could feel herself, and she didn't want that, either, and she found herself needing, with an intensity she had never imagined she would experience again, to make him understand that she didn't want to give him pain. Not him.

She went to him, her heart pattering, her feet soundless on the deep piled carpet, and she touched his shoulder, just tentatively, closing her eyes against the inrush of heady sensation produced by the feel of the warmth of him beneath the soft fabric of his shirt.

And that, the touching, had been a big mistake.

The caring caress of her fingers was like a match to a fuse and he stiffened for a heartbeat then swung round, gathering her in his arms, hungry for her.

Involuntarily, her own arms went up, clinging to him, feeling his need and shaken by it, and his mouth took hers, impatiently parting lips, his tongue sliding silkily into her mouth.

Tiah was floundering, drowning in sensation, her body fired by what he was doing to her with his hands, his mouth, by the scent of him, the feel of him beneath her clinging hands. And his hands moved, stroking her, discovering her, and she held him blindly, her body on fire with a thousand pulsating nerve ends wherever he touched.

'Tiah—you are so very beautiful . . .' There was a rasp in his voice, as if he found speech difficult, touch saying everything that was needed, and she tried to answer him, to tell him that this was a dreadful mistake, but her mind was foggy, hazed with the need he woke in her, and she couldn't form the words.

And when his mouth travelled moistly over the slender line of her throat, his fingers dealing swiftly with the tiny buttons on the front of her dress, his lips following like a starved man in search of sustenance, she forgot what she had been trying to say, gasping in intense excitement as he licked the tip of her taut breast, his hands moving to cup both, his mouth going from one to the other as if he could never have enough of either.

She moaned thickly, her need matching his, a fire out of control as she instinctively arched her body towards him, offering all she had to give, her fingers sliding down his lean body, feeling the hard curve of his rib-cage beneath almost unbearably sensitised fingertips, the warmth, the tight band of muscles about the waistband of his trousers.

'Oh God, Tiah—I want you so——' His hands shuddered down her flanks then pulled her close to the hardness of his body, a promise of what was now inevitable, before scooping her into his arms and carrying her to the wide sofa.

He was undressing her, his hands shaking, his eyes hazed with desire, and the sound of his breath as it came through slightly parted lips was ragged, matching her own. Tiah was naked now, except for a pair of lacy briefs, and as his fingers went to his shirt buttons she knew that what was about to happen was inevitable because she didn't want to fight it, even though she had promised herself it would never happen . . .

'We said this wouldn't . . . You said . . .'

She was incoherent, desire fighting common sense, common sense losing out even though she managed to make a token effort to swing herself upright. But his hands stayed her, the brief sharp flickering question in his eyes defeating her, and she collapsed in his arms, half laughing, half sobbing.

'This is crazy,' she gulped, her fingers stroking the wall of his chest as if they had a life of their own, out of reach of her will, feeling the steady pound of his heartbeat beneath the silk of his shirt, the warmth, the maleness of him. 'There's no way a platonic relationship between us is going to work out. We both know that. So—so maybe we should concede defeat, give in, stop seeing each other?'

'I never concede defeat.'

His voice was raw, and he meant that, she knew he did. She groaned, beyond help, as his hands cupped her face, his fingers tangling in the spilled mane of her hair as his eyes probed deeply into hers. Darkest blue absorbing silver, absorbing her . . .

'I want you, Tiah, as I've never wanted another woman. Believe me. I was already half in love with you the first time I saw you. And that was more than a year ago. So this isn't a new thing, not for me, and it isn't a light thing.'

Slowly, his hands dropped, his fingers feathering over the silky skin of her throat, splaying out to torment the taut globes of her breasts and his eyes never left hers, pulling her down into the swirling maelstrom of the desire that belonged to both of them, and Tiah knew she was lost.

CHAPTER FIVE

HE WAS kissing her deeply, lovingly, his hard body covering hers, and she knew that when she gave herself to him it would be with total commitment. No light thing for him, either, he had said so, and it frightened her.

Giving . . . Loving . . . It would mean complete and utter subjugation, as it had before, with Oliver. One life bound up with that of another, inextricably entwined, the bonds unbreakable, caught together with a dreadful interdependence that would go on, and on . . .

It could not happen again. She must not allow it to happen again.

And yet it was happening. Panicky, her fingers tightened in the thick softness of his hair where moments ago she had been holding him close, and she wrenched her mouth from beneath his, her mind fumbling with something he had said.

'You told me——' she gasped against his lean, tanned cheek, trying to ignore what his hands were doing, how he was making her feel. 'You told me you'd met me a year ago. I don't—don't remember our meeting. Tell me.'

His body stilled, as if a cold hand had been laid on him. 'Do we have to go into that now?' he muttered huskily, his lips finding the sensitive spot behind her ear.

Tiah jerked her head away, drowning, but clutching at straws.

'Yes—I want to know. Remind me.'

She knew they had never met before, she would have remembered. He had to be mistaken. But her insistence was a lever for prising them apart, for breaking the spell which was binding her closer and closer to him. She didn't have the strength to do it unaided. 'Tell me, Lucas.'

He grew very still, every muscle frozen until he lifted a hand to turn her head, his eyes holding hers with an intensity that turned her cold because she had seen that look before, in Oliver's eyes, and it brought memories back, slamming with painful recrimination into her mind.

He raised himself on one elbow, his eyes never leaving hers as he gently pushed the tumbled hair back from her face, the ball of his thumb stroking the slanting line of her cheekbone.

'You are more beautiful than I thought the first time I saw you,' he told her huskily. 'We didn't meet. But I saw you, and you've haunted me ever since.'

His fingers trailed slowly down the length of her neck, the fluid line of her shoulder, his eyes smouldering, almost black in the intensity of his harshly drawn features.

'God, how I've wanted you like this!' The words seemed torn from him, and Tiah stiffened. It couldn't happen twice in one lifetime, not this immediate recognition, the single-minded pursuit that brought inevitable capitulation. Such things couldn't happen twice. They couldn't!

'When did you first see me?' It hurt to speak, to breathe. Easier to give in to the enchantment of his hands, his lips, his body. Easier, but fatal.

'Not now, Tiah,' he groaned. 'Please not now!'

'*Now*'. Her eyes fought his, holding them with a strength she didn't know she had, and he told her, his words grating, almost savage,

'At your husband's funeral. You were leaving. I was passing. You didn't see me. You weren't seeing anything. But you've haunted me ever since.'

'I see.' Her mouth felt stiff, making speech difficult, her body becoming rigid instead of the clinging, moulding, melting thing of a few rapturous moments ago, and Lucas sighed, his eyes bleak and defeated.

She reached for the clothes which had been scattered heedlessly on the floor beside the sofa, holding her dress in front of her like a shield. She winced as he rolled away from her, reaching for his shirt, the atmosphere between them as cold as death itself, and bleak.

'That was one hell of a moment to choose to go into all that!'

'You brought it up,' she snapped back, defensively, glaring at him until he bit out, pain in his voice,

'And that was a damn mistake! I wanted to let you know that you weren't just a passing fancy. So I guess you could say that chivalry has its own rewards!'

She turned her eyes from the lean hard length of him, the angry movements as he thrust his shirt under the waistband of his trousers. The danger was gone, for the moment, but the thing that pulled them together would not lie dormant for ever—unless she killed it now. Stone dead.

Scrabbling into her own clothes, trying to force her mind along coherent channels, she heard the rough anguish in his voice. 'The last thing I want to do is pick a fight with you. Tiah—we have to talk, try to get a few things straight,' and knew what she could say to end it all, achieve a measure of safety for herself.

'But it's all been said, hasn't it?' Her voice sounded cool, but her shaking fingers betrayed her turmoil, and she cursed the dozen or so tiny fabric-covered buttons that refused to fit into corresponding buttonholes on the bodice of her dress.

And her words clipped savagely, in direct opposition to the flaccidity of her shaking hands.

'You saw me at Oliver's funeral and you fancied me. But being a man of at least *some* sensibility,' her voice derided, 'you allowed a decent interval to pass and then cooked up this exhibition thing. My work's not that good, and we both know it, but it gave you the opening you needed, didn't it? The bait, if you like. What I can't understand is why you told me where you'd first seen me—that bit of information was a cast-iron, guaranteed turn-off!'

She stuffed her feet into high-heeled sandals. He was completely still, watching her frantic movements. She didn't dare look him in the eyes, afraid of what she might see there, and she turned her back on him, looking for her handbag, whipping herself to fury because that was the only way she could continue this cruel killing of the thing between them—the thing that might have been beautiful.

'I suppose one dud exhibition could have been stomached,' she went on acidly. 'Not too bad a blow for the gallery's *fine* reputation.' She located her bag and her fingers closed tightly around the soft leather. 'I suppose you reckoned it was a reasonable price to pay. Or perhaps you would have cancelled it. October's a long time away. You would probably have tired of me before then.'

'Shut up!' His words bit, leaving a silence filled with waiting tension, and his fingers bit into the soft flesh of her arms as he forced her back on to the sofa. Tiah saw the implacable anger in his eyes, the whitening of his lips as he struggled to control the fury that had risen in answer to her own.

'Take me home!' There was a degrading wobble in her voice but her eyes were stormy and they locked unflinchingly with his and she knew they were bound together in a battle that would produce only one victor.

'Not before we've talked this out.' Lucas swung away, taking her untouched brandy from the table, putting the glass in her hands. 'Drink it. And stop writing scenarios for characters who don't exist. For some crazy reason you're doing your damnedest to start a fight. I'm not going to give you that pleasure, Tiah.'

He went to sit at the table, well away from her, and she could have laughed—or cried—because if he thought that by his keeping distance she had ceased to feel threatened by him, then he was out of his tiny mind!

'You asked where I had seen you first, and I regretted having mentioned it at all. But I'm never going to be less than honest with you, and so I told you—knowing full well what would happen. And as for that other wild accusation—you've done some fine work, and if you don't know it yet, you soon will. For that, and for no other reason, I offered you space at the gallery.'

His tone had changed, anger kept well at bay

now, and she recognised his tactics, shrugging
uninterestedly.

'So seeing a few pieces of my work around and
about was sheer coincidence!'

'Yes, dammit, it was!' The new gentleness in his
voice was rapidly disappearing. 'What do you take
me for? Some kind of wimp who has to invent
dubious ploys to get a woman's interest?'

Tiah gulped at her brandy, not really wanting it,
but it gave her something to do. His outburst had
shaken her because she knew it was justified. He
could get any woman he wanted, merely by
crooking a finger.

'I saw you, and you were beautiful. And I think
I fell in love with you, a little. But when I sought
you out it wasn't for that reason. I'm an adult
male, not an adolescent with his head stuffed full
with romantic fancies.'

He was speaking levelly, making every work
count, his tone almost impersonal. But Tiah knew
the tension was still there, knew that savagery lay
behind the smooth words—tightly leashed, but still
there.

'And when I saw you again I knew that what
had happened to me a year ago had been something
special. And, just as clearly, you showed me that it
was still too soon. And I promised——' his mouth
tightened, the flickering candlelight turning his face
to a hard mask, 'that I would ask nothing more
than friendship from you—for the time being. That
when we made love it would be because you
wanted it too.'

He drank his brandy in one gulp and slammed
the glass down on the table, his slitted eyes piercing
her, the derisory curl of his mouth making her
heart thunder, panic-stricken.

'And you did want me. And the biggest mistake I ever made was to try to reassure you, to let you know that you weren't a passing fancy for me because you'd been somewhere in the back of my head for a whole damn year! And you picked that up and used it as a bloody weapon to fight me off. Dammit, Tiah, I can make your body respond— but what about your heart?'

'I have no heart.' The words were torn wretchedly from her and she shuddered, feeling cold, so cold, and he moved swiftly, coming to sit beside her. 'Don't touch me!'

'I won't.' He sounded incredibly weary. 'You're quite safe with me.'

He was leaning forward, his hands dangling limply between his knees, his unreadable eyes holding hers in a long sideways look.

'You are young, talented, beautiful. So don't try to tell yourself that your heart died when Oliver died. Don't try to make yourself believe you've lost the capacity for love.'

His eyes still held hers and she tried to look away and couldn't. But her heart thundered a deep warning tattoo and she shuddered uncontrollably as he said huskily, 'You cloister yourself away from the real world, turn your home into a shrine to his memory—you long for the past, and the past's unattainable. Why? Because there's safety in that? Try to tell me.'

She couldn't speak. Panic was churning her stomach again, gripping her throat. He saw too much. She rubbed her hands together, feeling the dampness of her palms. His nearness, his caring, was getting through to her, touching her deeply. And she didn't want that. She made a conscious move to rise, but the look in those deep blue, steady eyes held her immobile.

'Why are you content to bury yourself away in that backwater, refusing human contact on any but the most superficial level, trying to hold on to the past? The past can't help you now. Only the present, and your acceptance of it, a willingness on your part to face the future, can do that. Besides,' his mouth quirked in the disarming manner that had fascinated her before, as he added drolly, 'you must find it mind-blowingly dull!'

She turned her head, hiding from those clever eyes. So he thought the pattern of her life must be dull, did he? Would the safe waters of a calm harbour be called dull by a lone seaman, limping to shore after enduring a battering storm at sea? She had found her safe anchorage after Oliver's death, had not found the tranquillity of it to be dull.

And now Lucas was threatening to drag her back into dangerous, turbulent waters . . .

'My life suits me fine,' she told him hoarsely, her fingers picking at the fabric of her skirts. 'Just fine. So don't try to push me into a mould of your making, to make me your creature—to follow your path instead of my own.'

'I would never try to do that.' His warm firm hand briefly covered hers, stilling the frantic, mindless movements of her fingers, and he removed it quickly, feeling the tension that shuddered through her body, turning it to brittle steel. 'But I do want to share things with you, and that means the past as well as the present and—hopefully, the future. Don't shut me out, Tiah. Tell me about your marriage. Was it so wonderful that even now you still can't tolerate the idea of another man ever taking his place?'

The sudden, unaccustomed humility in his tone tore her apart. There was no need for it. None at all. And had she been a different person, had a different life—a life which had not included Oliver—then she might have loved him as he had the right to be loved.

But she couldn't love, not again, and although she knew she could trust this man with her life there were things she could never share with him, with anyone, and her short marriage to Oliver was one of them.

She got unsteadily to her feet, her face ashen, blurting unthinkingly, 'You don't expect me to share the details of my life with Oliver with *you*, do you! And I think it would be as well if we forgot that wretched exhibition. I don't want to have to see you again.'

She felt his shock, his pain, even before he spoke, and when he did she knew, with an insight that left her feeling ill, that she was responsible for the death of something that could have been wonderful, had things been different.

'I take your point.' His voice was expressionless, his eyes stone. 'He must have been one hell of a guy. I'll take you home.'

She dreamed of Oliver that night and woke up sweating, her face grey, her mind blank with the numbing aftermath.

Yesterday, she had been a breath away from capitulating to Lucas's love-making, to her own needs, had already been committed to him in her mind.

She staggered out of bed, feeling a hundred

years old. For a time, a heady and rapturous time of losing herself in shared demands, shared needs and delights, held in Lucas's arms, Oliver had never been further from her mind.

But now he seemed to fill the house as last night he had filled her dreams, the ghostly echoes, the memories, of what had been between them pressing in, surrounding her, taking over, reminding her. If she hadn't already told Lucas that she didn't want to see him again then, after her dream-haunted night, it would have been first thing on her agenda this morning.

Rubbing herself down after a quick shower, she tried to make her mind a blank, shutting out all feeling, all emotion. And by the time she had zipped up her green cotton catsuit and twisted her hair into a loose knot on the top of her head she had almost achieved her objective.

Today was wet with a steady drizzle that might have kept her cooped up in the silent house, where the greyness of the day penetrated like the mist from the stream, if she let it. No point now in thinking about work for an exhibition. After last night's harrowing scene, that was definitely off. So she would do what she could to help Polly move into her cottage, relegating her own raw feeling to the back of her mind.

A sudden, unwanted image of how Lucas had looked—his mouth set in an unequivocal straight line, his eyes shadowed and hurting—rose to haunt her. She mentally pushed it aside with the brutal determination she knew she would have to rely on in the coming weeks when the pain of their parting— her own deliberately cruel misinterpretation of his words, his motives, had killed the thing that

had grown so quickly, so sweetly, between them—
would be at its keenest.

'You don't look well, dear.' Claudia's dark eyes
showed concern as Tiah joined her later in the
kitchen. Rain was running down the window, the
drizzle collecting in silvery droplets, and Tiah felt
the teapot under its patchwork cosy and dredged
up a smile.

'I'm OK. I overslept. It always makes me feel
like death.'

She poured her tea, evading Claudia's eyes,
shrugging when the older woman asked, 'Will you
be working today?'

'No point.'

'Oh?' A little, pregnant pause while Claudia
fussed around, putting bread in the toaster. The
sound of the vacuum cleaner, Polly at work in
another part of the house, covered the patter of
rain on the window. 'I imagined you would be kept
busy. For that so-called exhibition.'

'There isn't going to be one. Not of my work, at
least.' She took the slice of toast Claudia gave her,
buttered it and found she couldn't eat it. So she sat
staring at it while the butter melted, seeping into
the crisp brown surface, hearing the smiling
satisfaction in Claudia's words,

'Frankly, I'm pleased. I can see no point in
pushing yourself for something that can be of no
possible benefit. So what shall we do today? The
weather's too awful to do anything in the garden,
but we could drive into Compton and pick out
some material for that suit I promised to make
you.'

Claudia was an excellent needlewoman and the
suit had been promised for Tiah's birthday in

October, and now that Claudia knew the exhibition
was off she was painfully eager to make amends
for the sulkiness of the last few days.

'What have you got against Lucas Clent?' Tiah
pushed the toast away untouched. 'And why did
the thought of the exhibition upset you?'

'Against him?' Claudia's eyebrows rose, but
whether at Tiah's question or the uneaten breakfast
there was no way of telling. 'What could I have
against him? Now, shall we go to town? We could
choose the material and have lunch out. It would
make a nice change for us both.'

'Not today.' Tiah got to her feet. Edgy. Claudia
had neatly evaded her questions and was treating
her like a child, to be diverted by an outing. 'I
thought I'd give Polly a hand with the stuff from
the attics—that's if she's sorted anything out yet.'

'All manner of junk, I believe.'

If Claudia was disappointed she didn't show it
and Tiah guessed she was too relieved to hear the
exhibition had been cancelled to let anything bother
her at the moment. Though what she had ever had
against it Tiah couldn't imagine, and Claudia
obviously wasn't prepared to tell her.

Tiah could only guess that her sister-in-law had
seen it as something that would pull Lucas Clent
closer into their private little world, and Claudia
hadn't wanted that. It wasn't Lucas Clent she
objected to, personally. Any man who had
threatened to come between her and Tiah would
have been disliked. Well, Claudia didn't have to
worry about that. The closeness that had so quickly
developed between them had been shattered for
good.

'Why don't you go and have a word with Polly?'
Claudia suggested. 'She's already asked if she can

have two or three days off while she gets settled in. If you give her a hand she'll be back here with us so much the sooner.'

For the next three days Tiah was kept busy helping Polly move to her cottage, ferrying the smaller items over in her car while Joe hired a van to bring her brass bedstead, bedroom carpet and wardrobe from her old home.

'Everything else they can keep,' Polly said grudgingly as she and Tiah laid a staircarpet that had come to light in Deepdene's attics. 'The woman our Joe married'—she never referred to her daughter-in-law by her given name—'said as they couldn't afford to buy new furniture if I took all my stuff when I moved out and left the place to them. And just how she reckons I can, I'll never know!'

Her hat of the day, a stumpy arrangement covered with bit of an old feather boa, fell over her eye and she pushed it back irritably so that it perched on top of her head like a mad bird's nest.

'That's why I'm so grateful to you and Miss Claudia for all the things you've let me have.'

'We're only too glad you've found a use for it, Pol,' Tiah smiled, wiping a hand over her forehead, leaving a streak of dust behind. 'Better than leaving it to moulder away in the attic.'

'Oh ah.' Polly hoisted herself to her feet at the top of the stairs, her face red and shiny from her exertions. 'And talking about mouldering away, what's this I hear about you not showing your pictures like you'd arranged? Miss Claudia was real smirky about it—she'd like nothing better than to keep you hidden away, tied to her apron strings.

But I think it's daft. It would've taken you out of yourself, my girl.'

It had been days since she'd consciously thought of Lucas. By tacit agreement, neither she nor Claudia had mentioned the exhibition, or Lucas, and Polly's words had brought him back into her mind with a clarity that shocked her, twisted her up inside.

She turned her back, her mouth grim. 'There are still a few more boxes to fetch in from the car. I'll go and get them.'

Once she had unwittingly allowed him access to her mind she found it wasn't so easy to put him out again. And when Polly was settled in her cottage, and back in harness at Deepdene again, Tiah took to going for long and exhausting walks into the hills, wrestling with an inner confusion that never seemed to grow less, only more tortuous.

She should be thankful. She had had a narrow escape. She could so easily have fallen in love with Lucas and she had been spared the agony of that. Loving and losing had become two sides of the same coin, since Oliver.

But, as the days went by she was honest enough to admit that the initial thankfulness, engendered by panic, had, by some mysterious alchemy, emerged as a deep and aching regret. And her heart performed a wild dance of its own—one which she didn't stop to analyse—when, returning from a particularly long hike one late afternoon, Polly, on the point of departure, told her, 'That nice Mr Clent phoned a couple of hours ago. He said he wasn't going to take no for an answer, and if you hadn't got the guts to speak to him on the phone he'd come round here and make you. Or words to that effect.' Polly grinned, digging Tiah in the ribs with her well-padded elbow. 'I do like a masterful man! Oh——' she lowered her voice, moving closer, 'and I've written his home phone number down on a bit of paper and I put it in the tea caddy where she won't find it and rip it up.'

Unable to make much sense of that, or of her own instinctive pleasure in knowing that he wanted to contact her, Tiah hurried through to the kitchen. The phone number of his flat was where Polly had said it would be and she stared at the scrap of paper, smiling unstoppably, wondering at her own foolish response, but not wondering hard enough to do anything concrete about it—like shredding the paper and burning it and taking the phone off the hook and bolting the doors and pretending to be out when he called. As he inevitably would, if she didn't phone.

The idea of him coming here again both exhilarated and frightened her, and her fingers were shaking as she dialled his number.

And as the tone rang out she closed her eyes so that she couldn't see the combined and condemning stares of Oliver's painted eyes.

CHAPTER SIX

'So you finally deigned to phone me back.'

The roughness of his tone was tempered by an underlying warmth and a ridiculous wriggle of pleasure squirmed down Tiah's back and she gripped the receiver more tightly as if that could bring them closer together. Nevertheless, she was just about able to inject a note of sarcasm, 'I've only just got your message.'

'Come off it. I phoned three days ago, Tiah. I left a message with Claudia, asking you to contact me. Urgently. You didn't, and so I phoned again this afternoon.' He spoke with heavy patience, plainly disbelieving her. And that hurt.

'So what was so urgent it couldn't wait three days?' she countered witheringly.

'Nothing much. Just your future.' He was clearly having difficulty with his temper now and she felt oddly high, all at once, because he hadn't wiped his hands of her, after all. As he should have done, the way she'd acted, the things she'd said at their last meeting.

'I wanted to make sure that you don't chicken out of the exhibition,' he went on. 'Forget what happened the other night. Don't let that put you off. It wasn't important.'

There was a bleakness in his words that turned former elation to a cold heavy lump in her stomach, but what could she expect, after the way she had behaved? And his cool indifference was what she wanted, wasn't it? She closed her eyes against the irritating prick of tears as his voice clipped on, 'The only thing that is important is the exhibition. Important for me because I'd hate to think I'd frightened you off. For you, because it would be that first step forward to the recognition your work deserves.'

She heard him draw in a sharp breath and she could see, in her mind's eye, just how his face would look, thrown into harsh relief by the bleakness in him, the strong bones hard beneath the tanned skin, the mouth taut with impatience, the eyes inky, unreadable.

'Are you still there!'

The snapped words jerked her out of her reverie, tugging at some chord deep within her that would, she feared, always have her dancing mindlessly to his manipulation.

'Oh, just thinking it over.' She tried for lightness, a couldn't-actually-care-less tone that had him hopping mad, judging by his bitten, lightning response.

'Do more than bloody think! Are you, or are you not, going through with that exhibition?' And then, as an afterthought, a weary inducement, 'A purely business thing. No strings—not even one. You let enough slip the other night to get the message through my thick skull. But that can wait. All either of us need be concerned about at the moment is your work. So is the exhibition still on?'

'Yes.' And if he thought his rider had helped to make up her mind, then she couldn't help that because that was the way it must sound to him. He wasn't to know, and pride wouldn't let her tell him, that she had been regretting turning the space down almost as much as she had been regretting hurting him.

'Fine. We'll take it from there, then. And Tiah——' He had seemed about to hang up on her but after a momentary pause—during which time she got the impression that anything could happen now, that, somehow, her whole future relationship with this man swung on a pivot—he merely went on to say stonily, 'I'll be dropping by from time to time to see how you're progressing. And don't fly off at a tangent. My visits will be purely professional. Nothing else.'

She hadn't known she was capable of feeling so much relief. It was, so she assured herself, because of the exhibition. She hadn't wanted to lose that opportunity. Her work might be as promising as he had repeatedly said it was.

Also, and she had to give some credence to the other thought that pounded uncomfortably in her mind, she was glad he hadn't washed his hands of her. She hadn't truly wanted their short but stormy relationship to end on a sour note.

He had been truly generous with his encouragement as far as her work was concerned, and he had been kind, showing her a caring side of his nature that had touched her deeply—interspersed, of course, with the other more arrogant and infuriating and plain sexual side of his nature.

And at least, if he kept his visits few and strictly professional, they could both emerge from the encounter with some dignity. They could end up as more-or-less-friends. Nod pleasantly to each other if they happened to pass in the street, stop to ask about each other's doings, make some polite reference to the weather.

Over dinner she asked, very casually, as if it weren't of the least importance, 'Apparently, Lucas has been expecting me to phone him. He said he left a message with you three days ago.'

And Claudia looked up sharply, a dull flush staining her face, creeping up from her neck.

'I'm sorry dear. How forgetful of me. Have you been in touch? Was it important? Surely not?'

'It was, rather.' Tiah laid her cutlery down, wanting no more to eat because she knew forgetting a message from Lucas Clent was about the last thing Claudia would do.

She understood why. Claudia couldn't bear to think of her getting involved with another man. In her mind Tiah was still married to Oliver and would be until the day she died. Trying hard to keep her voice light and calm, she dropped her bombshell. 'It was about the exhibition. It's on again. Lucas and I must have got our wires crossed,' and watched as Claudia's flush receded, leaving her ashen, feeling sad that the older woman felt so much distress, but unable to do anything about it if she wasn't permitted to know why.

Tiah submerged herself in work, spending the long days in her studio or out in the hills with her painting gear. She had been worried that Claudia might start acting strangely again, guilty, because if she did Tiah knew it would be her fault.

But even after Lucas had called by, spending half an hour evaluating Tiah's progress, another half-hour having coffee with them both back in the house, Claudia had said nothing, done nothing.

Her wild accusations that Tiah was betraying Oliver by having anything at all to do with another man seemed, thankfully, to have been forgotten.

But there was a silent watchfulness about the older woman that would have worried Tiah had she allowed herself to dwell on it.

Instead, she threw herself into her work, her mind fully occupied with that, although a part of her was always on the alert to the possibility of another unheralded visit from Lucas.

Sure that he would come again, but not knowing when, ensured that her thoughts turned to him with a regularity she half deplored, half welcomed. There was a waiting quality about the long summer days, a tension that was strangely exhilarating, certainly not unpleasant, but keeping her stretched.

And one morning, when the wind scoured the skies to an impossible blue, she began a painting of a flower study, deep red and pink peonies, luscious, sleepily blowsy, casually arranged in a white porcelain bowl. Let him find some deeper, hidden meaning in this, she thought, grinning impishly, remembering his comment on the painting she had made of the bridge.

This memory, like many others she had, was oddly precious to her, keeping him near. Which was perverse of her, she decided resignedly, because his closeness, in the mind or in the flesh, was not something she actually wanted, was it?

And then he was there, his coming unannounced, standing in the open studio doorway, his black hair ruffled by the wind, his presence filling the room. Suddenly, the quiet surroundings were pulsating with the aura of his potent masculinity and, attuned to it as she always had been, Tiah reacted, tingles of unwanted and terrifying excitement burning their maddening way clear through her.

'How's it going?'

His voice was completely matter-of-fact, but his eyes seared her and she put her brush down, shamed by the colour she felt burn along her cheekbones, the husky quality of her voice as she inanely repeated, 'How's it going? OK, I think.'

One questioning look was all he gave her as he crossed to the work-bench where the three paintings he hadn't yet seen were propped, mounted but not yet framed. And she watched, unable to look away, as he stood in front of them, saying nothing.

He was wearing a fine wool shirt in dark brown, the sleeves rolled up to expose forearms which were more deeply tanned than ever. And she wondered if he had been away, to some exotic location. And if he had, with whom? She couldn't imagine him lying on a beach, windsurfing, whatever, on his own. Sudden jealousy dismayed her by its searing intensity, and she had no right to feel that way, because where he went, and with whom, had nothing to do with her.

Narrowly cut white trousers clipped long muscular legs, neat hips, and she felt her mouth go dry, the quivering, molten sensation in her groin an undeniable wanting—something that had no part in what she perceived of herself.

He still wasn't saying anything, and his silence, his effect on her, was unnerving. Outside, the branches of a shrub were blown in the wind, and she could hear them scraping and tapping against the studio window, but, louder than that, she could hear the thumping of her heart. She wondered if he could hear it too, and he turned, fathomless blue eyes locking with her troubled silver gaze.

'Well?'

'I——' Utterly confused now, both by the simmering silent rage she sensed in him and by her own deeply sexual reaction to him, she bit worriedly on her lower lip. Had that quiet anger of his anything to do with the quality of the work he had seen today? She could find no other reason for it.

'Is it hopeless?' She gestured jerkily to the work he had been so silently scrutinising. 'That lot, I mean.' Her eyes fixed on his unsmiling mouth then flickered shut, blocking out the sight of his inexplicable anger, even though she couldn't escape the sound of it.

'For heaven's sake! Have you no shred of confidence at all in your own work! Why put yourself down? Whatever or whoever makes you think it substandard?'

'Whoever' was nearer the mark. Oliver, and he had been a true artist, had never considered her work better than pretty daubs, her potential non-existent. But she couldn't tell Lucas that; it would seem as if she were putting a doubtful light on his judgment. The atmosphere between them was bad enough without that.

Besides, he, with his silent angry scrutiny, had engendered confusion, a brand of self-questioning that robbed her of serenity, stripped her down to the raw bones of the vulnerable creature she was. He had practically put those words in her mouth. It was his way, she had discovered—to undermine her conceptions of herself.

'Why are you so angry?' The words were dragged from her by the tight, ungiving lines of his face, the controlled rage that burned in his eyes, turning them black. He had been pleasant, polite, the last time he had been here. She couldn't understand this mood. It came near to hating. She shuddered convulsively, recalling all too vividly how it had felt to be held in his arms, how easily his hands and lips had brought her to the point of willing submission. Then he swung impatiently to the door, grinding out, 'If you haven't the imagination to make a damn good guess at what's eating me up, then I'm not laying myself open again by spelling it out!'

The weeks fled by, towards autumn, and Lucas didn't come again. On the surface, life went on the way it always had done since Oliver's death, with the quiet serenity that had been the hallmark of her days until Lucas Clent had erupted into her life, creating far-reaching ripples that had eroded her peaceful existence. Now the surface was placid again, but there were strong undercurrents below it, swirling, disrupting, dangerous.

She knew the work she was doing was good, because she believed him now, and she strove to make it better, becoming more critical of it than ever, forcing herself to work as she had never worked before.

Claudia, thank heavens, seemed reconciled to the fact of the exhibition, although she never mentioned it, and she spent her days quietly, busy in the garden—which was her passion—or with her needlework; pleasant, gently concerned if she thought Tiah was working too hard, pushing herself. But there was something beneath the surface there, too, and although Tiah couldn't put her finger on it, it worried her.

And sometimes, when she couldn't sleep and lay listening to the hoot of the owls, the sigh of the wind, the endless murmuring of the stream, or when she dare not sleep because of the dreams of Oliver which were coming to her at increasingly frequent intervals, she thought of Lucas, turning her mind to him as though she could reach him that way. And she thought of the way he had seemed, of the anger in him, of the things he had said.

She knew now that he wouldn't drop by, in a professional capacity, or otherwise. And she accepted that, knowing instinctively that their time of reckoning would come—in one form or another—but it wouldn't be yet.

His wanting, his frustration, had been mirrored by his anger and she knew she wouldn't see him again until he had accepted the fact that she could never be his. Not wholly. Or until she went to him, which she could never do because her life with Oliver had made her unfit for any other man, unable again to make the full and lasting commitment of love.

Towards the end of September she knew she could do no more towards the exhibition. She had worked herself out. But time stretched before her, a vacuum that could not now be filled, as it had been so easily and comfortably before. The pleasurable pursuits of work in the garden, or about the house, long hours of reading—or anything else—held no appeal now.

Even Claudia's company, her unfailing devotion, became an irritant. Tiah felt guilty about that but could do nothing to alter it. Such unstinting affection could be smothering, and maybe she should think again about moving out, finding a place of her own, impressing on Claudia that the need for independence didn't mean a lessening of affection, a breaking of family ties.

Deciding that a long walk in the hills might do something to subdue the restlessness that filled her, the sense of being confined, suffocated, she dressed in faded black denim jeans, comfortable shoes and a jade lambswool sweater. She told Claudia she wouldn't be in until dinner and marched across the bridge and up the incline, determined to unwind.

At the turn-off she veered left, along the road that dwindled to a track, leading nowhere in particular, striding loosely, filling her lungs with the sweet sharp air, drinking in the early autumn colours and at last feeling herself begin to relax.

The sound of an approaching car, coming from behind her, had her walking on the overgrown verge, allowing plenty of leeway, and all those feelings of incipient relaxation vanished, exploding into mind-bending tension as the vehicle halted and Lucas said drily, 'I was on my way to Deepdene but saw a lone figure up ahead. I recognised that determined stride. Hop in.'

And why not? she thought, pleasure taking the place of tension because he seemed glad to see her and she was glad to see him.

But, 'What did you want to see me about?' she prevaricated, his presence, her happiness at seeing him confusing her, muddling her mind. And she knew it showed, that he was reading her like a book, getting inside her head, because his smile was quirky, one eyebrow very slightly, humorously raised as she babbled on, 'You must want something, if you were on your way to Deepdene.'

'Just to see you.' He leaned over the passenger seat and swung the door open, grinning, 'Come on, get in. I promise I won't bite.' And she got in because she didn't know what else to do; he had her mesmerised, she thought sourly. And he was still grinning, damn him, as he drew away and idled down the track, looking for somewhere to turn.

'Where were you going?'

'Just walking.' Were, she noted crossly. As if his arrival, the fact that he wanted to see her, automatically cancelled any plans she might have made.

'Making a day of it?'

'Yes.' She tried to fan her annoyance but she was having difficulty with her mouth. She wanted to keep it stiffly disapproving, but it had ideas of its own, it seemed, and wanted to break into a grin to match his own.

'Good.'

And what he meant by that she had no idea, but whatever it was he was looking smugly pleased with himself, totally relaxed. They had long passed the turn-off to Deepdene before she found the wits to ask, 'Where do you think you're taking me?' and he turned his head and gave her a smile that melted the last feeble hope of resistance utterly, made her feel happier than she could remember, carefree enough—even though her heart did lurch uncomfortably—to take his reply in her stride.

'To see my mother. I don't get on with her, by the way. But don't let that throw you, we're always very civilised when we do meet. I decided it was time I introduced her to the woman I intend marrying.'

'Oh.' Tiah digested this in silence, then came up with, 'We're picking her up somewhere, are we?' Her voice was tart, but not as tart as she had intended it to be because the bubble of laughter inside her had got in the way.

'You know who I mean, Tiah. So don't pretend you don't.'

There was wry amusement in his tone and it warmed her, and she closed her eyes, leaning back against the headrest. Seeing him again, being with him like this, had brought a peace of mind she hadn't believed attainable, an accepting happiness that was in sharp contrast to the edgy striving of the time since she'd seen him last.

She had believed he wouldn't attempt to see her until he had come to terms with her intrinsic withdrawal, but it seemed she had been wrong. And his mood was good, not bitingly angry as it had been at their last meeting, and she wasn't about to ruin it. She would relax, enjoy his company, and think about the implications of what he had said some other time—when she felt stronger-minded. And try not to think of how it had been, in his arms, when mutual passion had consumed them both, pushing them to the brink.

'I've spent a lot of time thinking over the past few weeks,' he imparted, his voice easy and assured against the expensive purr of the engine. 'And I came to the unpalatable conclusion that I was losing my grip. I've always known where I was heading, known what I wanted. But you threw me, you really did. You got me believing I was a loser, for the first time ever. And losing doesn't suit me, Tiah.'

He shot an enquiring look at her, laced with amusement, but her profile might have been carved from stone.

She noted the pause, felt his eyes on her and had to exert complete control to stop the laughter inside from escaping. She didn't need him to tell her that the mantle of a loser wouldn't sit comfortably on those broad shoulders of his. She had known that instinctively, the first time they'd met. But he was talking about her, about marriage, and she knew she should come up with some cutting remark, demand he turn the car right round and take her home. Now.

But she was tired of shutting herself away inside herself. Tired of the lack of laughter, of dream-haunted nights that coloured her days black. And she enjoyed his company and she was honest enough to admit that she was exhilarated by the electrifying sexual tension between them. And she enjoyed his moods, good or bad, and she would indulge herself, just for today.

'So I'm giving you fair warning of my intentions,' he was telling her. 'So far, I haven't had time for a permanent relationship—marriage——'

'And now you have?' she put in drily, her silvery eyes flickering sideways, completely disconcerted by his grinned response,

'Married to you, it would be the other things in my life I would have to try to make time for.'

There was nothing she could say to that, the mental picture his words had picked out of the air brought hot colour to her cheeks and she turned her face to the window, staring at the blur of the passing hedgerows as if she had never seen such things before.

'I'm in love with you. I love you.' His words dropped lightly into the silent space and her spine stiffened with the shock of hearing them—just like that.

He sounded casual, but immensely sure of himself. 'I won't make a big production of it, and I don't expect you to, either. I just want you to know that I'm going to marry you—and that I'm not setting a time limit on how long it takes for you to come to understand that you want it, too.'

'How masterful! What are you—the last of the chauvinists?' Her words dripped with sarcasm. She had to think of it as a sick joke, or try not to think of it at all—which would be much better but rather difficult. To take him seriously would mean that she would have to take her own feelings for him seriously, too. And there was no point in that, particularly as she didn't know what they were.

She sneaked a look at his profile, catching her breath because his male beauty got to her, it really did, and the male-female awareness between them was tangible, she could feel it, growing, always growing, binding them yet threatening to tear them to pieces.

Trying to deflect it, she asked coolly, 'Why don't you and your mother get on? Or is that none of my business?'

'Let's say we're incompatible.' His eyes flickered sideways, impaling her. 'Anything to do with me is your business, as from now. I won't be the one to sour our relationship by keeping things hidden.'

Which was a dig at her and her refusal to talk about Oliver, her marriage. Her sable lashes dropped, fixing on the fingers that had clenched together in her lap, aware of the effort he was making to keep the atmosphere easy.

'She made my father's life hell on earth, and I don't think I'll ever forgive her for that. She left him for another man. There was a divorce. But he never stopped loving her, even though she went through two husbands after him. She came crawling back after her third husband died—number two had divorced her—and ended up without a penny. My father bought the cottage she lives in now, provided for her. I took on that particular burden, too, after Father died.'

'I'm sorry.' Tiah's eyes were soft with compassion. She knew what it was like to come from a broken home, the feeling of rootlessness, of not really belonging anywhere. But his wide hard shoulders lifted in a barely perceptible shrug.

'Don't be. I can well afford my mother's upkeep.'

'I didn't mean that.' Her mouth straightened at his callous remark. 'I meant the break-up of your parents' marriage.'

'Again, there's no need. I'm not angling for sympathy. The person to be pitied was my father, but he's out of it now. It didn't affect my life.' There was a hardness in his voice that turned her cold. 'I didn't let it. I thought we were well rid of her, in any case. Until I was around six I thought we were a normal happy family. I suppose I just took it for granted, the way kids do. There were no loud quarrels, nothing to give me a clue. Then she just left. After that, things got back to normal pretty quickly for me. Aunt Blanche, Father's elder sister, moved in and took Mother's place more than adequately. I didn't suffer in any way—they saw to that.'

But surely a little boy of six must have suffered when his mother left, Tiah thought, staring at his enigmatic profile. Though to listen to him talk of that time the only detectable emotion was a certain detached callousness.

And that didn't tie in with what she knew of him. Perhaps she didn't know him as well as she thought she did. She shivered, remembering. Did anyone really ever know another person?

They had passed through Compton and were in open country again; Lucas slowed the car as they

approached a village and he grinned, breaking the
atmosphere which had been beginning to grow
thick with unease.

'Dothington. The archetypal English village. A
touch twee for my tastes.'

And for hers, Tiah had to acknowledge as they
passed the painstakingly picturesque village green,
the mandatory black and white thatched cottages,
the well groomed churchyard at the side of the
small Norman church. He pulled into a drive at
the side of one of the cottages, the immaculate
garden aflame with scarlet dahlias, and Tiah
mumbled, suddenly frightened by the implications
of what he was attempting to do in bringing her
here, 'I'm not dressed for visiting.'

'You're beautiful.' His eyes derided her feeble
protest. 'Mother's expecting us for lunch.'

'Sure of yourself, weren't you,' she uttered
crossly, leaving the car as he did because there was
nothing else for it, not now, and he smiled at her
over the long blue bonnet, the metal glittering in
the sunlight.

'Naturally. I told you, I don't figure myself for a
loser—especially where you're concerned.'

The yapping of a pair of rough-haired terriers
betrayed their arrival, and there was no backing
out now because a small, artfully fluffy woman
appeared in the dogs' wake, and all Tiah could do
was hope and pray Lucas hadn't told his mother
that he was bringing his intended wife to meet her.
It would make things impossibly difficult. She had
no intention of marrying again.

Introductions were made. 'Call me Ellie,' his
mother said, 'everyone does.'

And after that everything was pleasant, on the
surface, and if there was antagonism between

mother and son it didn't show. And after lunch Ellie suggested a tour of her garden.

'It's only half an acre but it keeps me out of mischief. It's my main preoccupation these days.'

'I've a couple of phone calls to make,' Lucas bowed out. 'You don't mind, Ellie?'

'How could I? When you pay the bills?' Her eyes, a greyer blue than her son's, smiled at Tiah as she spoke to Lucas. 'You can safely join us in the summer house in half an hour. I shall have finished boring Tiah by then.'

But Tiah wasn't bored. The garden was beautiful, perfectly maintained, and she said so, touched by the older woman's ingenuous pleasure at her praise, and any thoughts of possible boredom disappeared completely when Ellie, settling herself on one of the wicker chairs in the summer house, said, 'You can't imagine how happy it's made me to meet you. Lucas has never introduced me to any of his lady-friends before, and you've no idea how that has hurt, over the years. Mind you, he's never before considered marrying one of them, so perhaps it's not too surprising.'

'He told you that?' Tiah was stunned. She had hoped, believed, that what he had said had been private, something to be resolved between the two of them. Bringing it out into the open made it seem real, frighteningly so. Perhaps that had been his intention—to force her to face his determined intention to marry her. He was clever enough to manipulate events to his own advantage.

'Yes, I'm glad to say he did. We have never been as close as I would have liked.' Ellie patted her tinted fluffy hair, smoothing it back from her expertly made-up middle-aged face. 'It's given me hope. Maybe he is at last learning to forgive me.'

'Forgive you?' Tiah echoed hollowly, looking across the garden, hoping for Lucas, because this conversation was full of uncomfortable undertones. But there was no sign of him, and Ellie said scathingly, 'Yes, forgive and forget. He's a grown man now and should be able to see things through an adult's eyes.'

'Lucas strikes me as being completely adult,' Tiah came back tartly, not wondering, yet, at her instinctive defence of the man who threatened her peace of mind, destroyed her serenity, had given— quite literally—the kiss of life to emotions she had believed dead.

'Oh absolutely,' Ellie remarked coolly. 'But he can display the callousness of a six-year-old at times.'

A six-year-old? Something cold and sharp twisted inside Tiah. Lucas had been six when his mother had left. He had told her it hadn't affected him. But it must have done. The split-up between Tiah's parents hadn't caused her much more than a passing sadness in later years. She had been only a few months old at the time. And life at boarding-school had suited her and she had accepted it because it had been the only life she had known. She had never had a real home, the support of loving parents—but to be deprived of a mother at six years old must have had a traumatic effect.

Was something dark and tormented about to be brought into this golden autumn day, something that would explain his previous inability to make a lasting emotional commitment? Something more credible than his own explanation of lack of time?

If so, Tiah didn't want to know. Whatever it was, it belonged to him, to his past, and delving into another's past only brought people closer, gave an insight that only the closest of relationships could stand up to. She didn't want that. Wasn't ready for it, doubted if she ever would be.

But something about Ellie's complacent features told her she wasn't going to be able to evade the issue.

'Not that he hasn't been a dutiful son since his father died; he has,' Ellie was saying, her shallow mind unruffled by the darkness Tiah sensed lurking behind the light words, the pretty, ageing face. 'He continues to support me, as his father did. He visits—for roughly half an hour—each month to collect the bills and bring my allowance. But he doesn't forgive me for leaving his father. Thirty years on, and he can't forget.' The greyish eyes widened. 'Can you credit that?'

'I don't really know,' Tiah countered distantly. 'And maybe you shouldn't be talking to me like this.'

'And why not? It's not often I get the opportunity to talk to someone who could help me get closer to that son of mine. I expect he told you about the divorce?' And, as Tiah dipped her head in reluctant acknowledgment, 'So what's new? Lucas didn't suffer. He had an agreeable life. A father who adored him, a comfortable soul—his aunt—to take my place. But children are self-centred creatures, aren't they? Only thinking of what they want.' Ellie made a little helpless gesture with her hands, not looking at Tiah now as she continued, 'He was fifteen years old, I remember, when he told me he never wanted to set eyes on me again. Imagine, and I was his mother! I had married a Frenchman, but it didn't work out and after the divorce I came back to England and told my first ex that I wanted to see my son, get to know him again. I had such a pleasant time planned, I was staying at a London hotel and Lucas was to join me for a couple of weeks and we were to see the sights and have a fun time. He arrived, a gangly schoolboy trying to act like a grown man. He informed me—in that cold, detached way of his—that he had come because his father had insisted, but he was getting the next train home. He wasn't staying. He was rejecting me as I had rejected him. Those were his very words,' she sniffed, then added petulantly, 'I called him a prig, I recall, and he called me a name I won't repeat.' She shuddered fastidiously and Tiah could have hit her.

'And then it all came tumbling out—how he had been at home on the day I left his father for Marcel. Lucas had been off school—measles, or some such. And apparently, he had heard raised voices in the hall and had got out of bed and crouched on the stairs in his pyjamas. His father had pleaded with me not to leave—I can hear his voice still. But it wasn't any use, how could it be? I had stopped loving him and would only have made him even more miserable had I stayed. Besides, why should I have given up my chance of happiness with Marcel? Surely it was better that I went—anyone would have been able to see that. Anyway, Brian—Lucas's father—told me to think carefully. I had a choice to make, between him and our son, or Marcel. And Lucas overheard,' she sighed pitifully. 'And he has never forgiven me for making the only choice I could.'

Bow out, stage left, Tiah thought waspishly. And bring on the violins!

Emotion choked her throat, surprising her by its sheer intensity as she thought of the scars of rejection this light-minded woman had inflicted thirty years ago. How could any woman leave her child—her sick child—and expect no lasting effects?

And her heart went out to the man who had been the child, the rejected child who had become the gangly youth who had, in his turn, rejected. And she knew, with a pain that tore her to shreds, that she loved the man.

But it was a love which could not be given the freedom to grow. It could never be openly acknowledged because of the memories of what Oliver had been to her.

CHAPTER SEVEN

'WELL, you're off then.' Polly's little bright black eyes approved Tiah's belted deep blue fine wool coat, her elegantly coiled hair. 'Best of luck, then!'

Polly was acting as if this were a momentous occasion. And Tiah supposed it was, in a way.

'I'm only going to check if my paintings are hanging the right way up!' she grinned.

Someone from the gallery had come in a van yesterday to transport her work, the framed paintings already wrapped in clean sacking for protection, to Compton. Their own staff would hang the pictures, Lucas had told her, and she could supervise the operation, or not, as she pleased.

Tiah had thought it best to leave them to it, they were the experts, and today, the opening of her exhibition, she was going along to view the result.

She pulled on black kid gloves and Claudia poked her head round the kitchen door. 'May I come with you?'

'But of course!' Tiah was frankly astounded. Claudia had not once referred to the exhibition since Tiah had told her it was on again. She could hardly believe she had relented enough to actually want to see it!

'I'm ready when you are.' Claudia was looking her best in a dove-grey light tweed suit, but there

was a certain twitchiness about her that Tiah tried
to dispel as soon as they were on their way.

'We could have lunch somewhere after we leave
the gallery. That Italian restaurant in Book Street
is good.'

'Oh, but I'm not going to the gallery,' Claudia
disclaimed quickly. 'I shall visit the park. But lunch
would be nice. We can meet up when you've
finished.'

So much for taking an interest, Tiah thought
drily. Claudia would never admit that she had a
life of her own, a career which might hold more
possibilities than the occasional commissioned
portrait of someone's pet!

Claudia fell silent, apparently lost in contem-
plation of the passing countryside, and Tiah
concentrated on her driving and wondered whether
Lucas would be at the gallery, to see her work, or
if he had little interest in the finished result once
the artist's work had been vetted and the practical
arrangements been made.

She hadn't seen him or heard from him since he
had driven her back from his mother's five days
ago. He had been charming, amusing, utterly at
his ease, not guessing, fortunately, at the thoughts
that had been tormenting her ever since that
blinding, shocking realisation of her love for him.

She had been extremely careful of those thoughts,
containing them, not wanting to give him a single
clue to the way she was feeling, thankful that he
seemed content to keep their conversation on a
light, easy level. She didn't know whether she
would have been able to handle the situation had
he again spoken of loving her, of his intention to
marry her.

The days since seeing him last had been empty,

but empty days could be filled, she told herself grimly. But she longed for him with a primitive need that appalled her, loved him with an aching intensity that frightened her silly. She knew what love could do, and had the scars to prove it.

One thing though, was quite apparent: she would never willingly see him again unless it was unavoidable. It was the only sensible course of action. And if the unavoidable happened she would have to make him understand that he must put her out of his mind before they both got badly hurt. She didn't want to hurt him, not him, and she wouldn't put herself through the same agony twice. Because even though she loved him, she couldn't marry him. Marriage to Oliver had contained enough to last her through her life.

She left Claudia at the main park gates after promising to meet her back there in an hour, watching the older woman walk through the gates, holding herself stiffly as if any slight relaxation of the tautly held limbs could result in total uncontrol.

Parking the car further down, where the road widened, Tiah walked the short distance to the gallery, almost calm. She loved Lucas, but would get over the sweet pain of it. She had loved and lost before. And had recovered.

But recovery was well delayed as she started to climb the stairs to the exhibition rooms to meet him clattering down. He stopped when he saw her and his whole body was tense with anger.

'I was just on my way to phone you.' The hard words came out through his teeth and her breath caught in her throat with nameless apprehension, and she wanted to cry because she loved him so much.

'Oh?' Composure was difficult to maintain. His

wintry eyes froze her. And the muted rattle of
china, the faint aroma of coffee rising from the
rooms below, came to taunt her. The woman she
had been, a few short months ago, drinking coffee
with a man she was so sure she could dismiss, was
a world apart from the raw, vulnerable creature
she had become.

And was their relationship to end like this—in
open hostility on a flight of polished oak stairs?
She didn't want that—oh, how she didn't!

She raised misty searching eyes, troubled eyes.
There was a bitter savagery about him she had
never encountered before, not even in him, and
she moistened her lips, her voice scarcely above a
whisper,

'What's wrong?'

'You can honestly ask me that—and not know!'
He was making some effort to control his anger,
she could tell he was, but his fingers were flexed,
his knuckles white. As if he could do murder.

'I invited you to show your paintings. Not
Oliver's.' He flattened himself against the wall,
gesturing, 'After you,' and Tiah walked on up, not
looking at him, feeling the colour drain from her
face, her knees shaking. She didn't know what he
was talking about, but could make a damn good
guess.

'Len hangs the paintings. He phoned me an hour
ago, he said he thought he had what appeared to
be a foreigner in with your work.' His voice came
from right behind her, low and deadly. 'I took one
look and told him to take it down.'

They had reached the small vestibule at the head
of the stairs and he stopped her, moving in front of
her to block her entry, his mouth compressed.

'I am not an idiot, Tiah, so don't try to treat me

like one. If you want to put your late husband's work on show—find some other venue. Don't try to sneak it in here under my nose. I suggest you take it back with you when you leave, otherwise I might be grossly tempted to throw it out for the garbage collectors. Understand?'

Her mouth was too dry with dread to answer. So that was why Claudia had spared her further acid comments on the subject of her coming exhibition. She had obviously taken the opportunity to smuggle one of Oliver's canvases in with the batch of watercolours Tiah had put ready for collection. Protectively wrapped, as they all had been, no one would have noticed until they came to be hung. There was no other explanation.

Her hands curled into tight fists at her sides as she met his accusing eyes. She could kill Claudia for putting her in this impossible situation, she really could! Throttle her with her own bare hands—but she could never betray her. She was sick, troubled, and in need of understanding, not censure.

And there was more than accusation in his storm-blue eyes. There was naked pain, and it hurt her deeply, but she couldn't make explanations, betray Claudia's sickness. It was too frightening, and she was too loyal.

Her face was ashen, her skin pulled tight, making her delicately structured facial bones seem brittle and hard, and her voice came out cold as a chiming bell as she pushed past him.

'I'll take it away now.'

It was a particularly stark portrayal of human conflict. Two sexless, naked figures locked in violent combat, depicted in harsh brush strokes, angry colour. Tiah had always disliked this canvas.

During the last months of his life Oliver had seemed obsessed with violence.

She lifted the canvas from where it was propped against a wall and Lucas said, 'I'll carry it for you, to your car,' and she relinquished it, her fingers nerveless, her mind preoccupied with what must have been going on inside Claudia's head when she had taken this painting down from the large dining-room wall where it had hung since Oliver's death. She would have hurried with it, anxious not to be seen, over to the studio, wrapping it, pushing it in with the others. If Tiah's inferior daubs were to be put on public display, then something of Oliver's deserved a place, too.

Sighing defeatedly, Tiah followed Lucas back down the stairs, her eyes dwelling on the proud set of his head, the breadth of his shoulders beneath the soft tan suede jacket he wore.

On the pavement he turned, his features set.

'Where have you parked your car?'

'It doesn't matter. I can manage.'

'I said,' the words came tightly, through clenched teeth, *'where is your car?'*

She gave in after that, eaten by hopeless misery. He was angry, savagely so, and she couldn't blame him. He would have been justifiably annoyed if anyone else had pulled such a trick. But he believed that the woman he loved, the woman he had stated he intended to marry, had tried to sneak her dead husband's work in under his nose. She felt his pain as if it were her own. It was her own. And she could do nothing to ease the situation for either of them.

The canvas fitted into the boot of her car and as he handed her back the keys the lines of tension that hardened his face, the hurt that darkened his eyes, flayed her. Now was the moment to tell him that he must put her out of his mind, forget her. After the little episode with Oliver's canvas it shouldn't be too difficult to convince him that she was bad news as far as he was concerned.

He had said he loved her, and she believed him. This morning's sorry, sick charade would hardly be causing him so much grief if he didn't care about her deeply. And she didn't want to hurt him, not in the way he was hurting now, and never seeing each other again was the best thing either of them could do.

She moistened her lips to tell him so, her anguished eyes imprinting his features on her mind for one last time—the rich copper lights the thin sunlight picked from his dark thick hair, the strength and beauty of that masculinely sculpted face, the drowning depths of his eyes . . .

'Tiah . . .' His voice was husky with emotion, the hand that lightly and lovingly reached out to touch her face, so gentle, saying so much more than words ever could. 'I'm sorry. So sorry.'

She closed her eyes against her pain, the exquisite sensations engendered by his touch, the awe-inspiring thought that this big, gentle man was sublimating his own hurt anger because he felt her pain. The pain was there, and it was hers all right, but it wasn't derived from the source he believed it was.

He cupped her upturned face in both hands, the balls of his thumbs softly brushing away the tormented tears that escaped her closed eyelids, and she gasped as she felt the tender touch of his lips against hers, groaning deep in her throat as unstoppable love for him, hunger for him, engulfed her in an aching tide.

And her lips parted beneath his in instinctive, primal invitation, and as the tip of his tongue slid silkily around the quivering softness of her open lips she melted against him, lost in her love for him, her arms reaching up to twine around his neck, heedless of passers-by.

Lucas moaned his answering need, a shudder ripping through his lean hard body, transmitting the heated vibration to her clinging flesh, and he lifted his head, his eyes hazed with desire, regret, as he untwined her hands with his own.

'Any more of this and we're liable to get arrested,' he said thickly, running unsteady raking fingers through his hair, his eyes holding hers, the heated promise in them shocking her because she knew it negated the promise she had made to herself as Oliver died.

She couldn't tell him to forget her. She couldn't inflict that kind of pain on either one of them, and the knowledge sobered her. It was quite an admission, and one she would need to think long and seriously about.

'Let's have some lunch, Tiah.'

He took her hand, smiling down at her, and underneath the warmth she detected a longing, a triumph she couldn't blame him for. He was winning, and he knew it, but he didn't know how complete his victory was. And that was something else she would have to think about. Think coldly and analytically, some time later. She wasn't capable of coherent thought when his nearness, the open adoration in his eyes, the secret love in her own heart, all combined to drive the past back to a place where it was beyond recognition.

'I can't—I——' Tiah floundered, flushed, confused and dismayed by the plummeting depths of her disappointment. Her troubled silvery eyes held his, verifying her regret. 'I said I'd meet Claudia for lunch. She came in with me.'

'Fine. So I take you both to lunch.' He tucked her hand through the crook of his arm and patted it. A world of gentle reassurance there. 'Just the two of us, and I probably wouldn't be able to eat a thing. I'd be too busy thinking of satisfying a very different appetite. Claudia can act as a chaperon! Where are we meeting her?'

Bemused, ridiculously happy, Tiah told him, 'At the park gates.' She looked at her watch, blurrily. 'About now.'

'Then we'd better get going.'

They walked hand in hand and Tiah's heart lurched drunkenly, her entire consciousness confined to the touch of skin on skin, his stronger, longer fingers entwined with hers, transmitting sensations that turned her blood to fire. And it wasn't until she saw Claudia's patient, upright figure at the park gates that dread clutched icily at her heart, making it pound.

Fearful of her sister-in-law's reaction to seeing her with Lucas, Tiah swallowed nervously, her fingers clutching at his hand, her skin crawling with heat despite the autumnal nip in the bright crisp air. And Claudia began to advance towards them, her dark eyes fixed on their clasped hands.

'Well, and how did your exhibition look?' The query was light, interested, the smile entirely pleasant. 'How nice to see you again, Mr Clent.'

Tiah's body tensed and she pulled her hand from his clasp. Relief warred with an unaccustomed anger against Claudia. She had sneaked Oliver's canvas in with the rest, had made her, Tiah, look a fool and worse, the devious ploy hurting Lucas

more than he had admitted—and she could still
stand there, looking like everyone's favourite aunt—
and act as if she didn't know what she had done!

Claudia's question hovered on the air and Tiah
couldn't answer it. She hadn't given her work a
single glance. But Lucas didn't realise that the
question wasn't an entirely normal expression of
interest and he answered for her, skirting round
the perimeters of Tiah's distress, though completely
mistaking the reason for it.

'It looked good. Bound to be a great success.
So, to celebrate, I'm taking you both to lunch.'

His easy charm set the tone for the next two
hours, and if Tiah hadn't known better she could
have believed that Claudia was entirely won over
by his warmth. But she did know better and could
detect the quickly veiled antagonistic expression of
those dark eyes, the momentary flaring of elegant
nostrils.

But there again, those physical manifestations of
an unaccountable but deep-seated dislike were so
slight, so well hidden that only Tiah, with her
emotion-heightened perception, could detect them.
The surface was unruffled, the appreciation of good
food and wine apparently sincere. If Tiah were to
try to tell Lucas of Claudia's precarious mental
balance—not that she would think of so demeaning
the woman who had until lately been so kind, so
supportive—he simply would not be able to believe
her.

Tiah ate little and contributed even less to the
ongoing flow of easy conversation. She was totally
absorbed in watching Lucas now, his long, finely
made fingers resting on the stem of his wine-glass,
his head tilted just slightly to catch what Claudia
was saying, but his eyes, deeply, brilliantly sapphire

beneath the curve of sooty lashes holding her own, snatching her breath away as she coped with the sudden curling ache in the pit of her stomach.

There was something very special growing between them, something shining, like light. It reached out from him and surrounded her, permeated the surface of her skin, suffused her, and she welcomed it knowingly, honestly, almost sure, now, of the outcome.

'This has made a delightful change, Mr Clent.'

Lucas had walked them back to Tiah's car and Claudia was at her most gracious.

'I have enjoyed it.' Her dark eyes swept assessingly over the tall man's lithe body in a way that turned Tiah cold, though she couldn't have said why. 'Perhaps you would allow me to repay your kindness?' Dark eyes swept to Tiah's, held, then slipped away. 'It's Tiah's birthday in three days' time. We would both like it so much if you could come to dinner on Thursday. Seven-thirty?'

His eyes narrowed as he registered Tiah's involuntary gasp of dismay. She didn't want to see Lucas there, in the house that had been Oliver's home for all his life, where the presence of him still clung, tenaciously, all-pervasively, as he had vowed it would. And she couldn't believe that Claudia wanted it either, but there was nothing she could do or say as Lucas accepted smoothly.

'I shall look forward to that. Seven-thirty on Thursday, then,' and to Tiah, clever blue eyes denying her the strength of mind it would take to look away, 'I'll be in touch with you before then.'

'Why did you invite Lucas to dinner?'

Tiah had difficulty keeping her voice casual to

the point of indifference, but she managed it, just
as she had managed to negotiate the traffic-clogged
Compton streets. But now they were on open
country roads and she could relax her concentration
enough to question Claudia. 'Have you changed
your mind about my seeing him?'

It was a forlorn hope, stillborn as Claudia ignored
the question, saying softly, 'I had forgotten how
much Oliver and I used to enjoy the park. Strolling
around, feeding the ducks on the lake, was quite
like old times.'

'Claudia!' Tiah gritted her teeth. There were
things that had to be sorted out, no matter how
unpleasant. 'I have one of Oliver's canvases in the
back of the car. Why——?'

'Oh?' Dark eyes flickered, clouded. 'Why bring
it away? Why didn't you leave it there, with the
others?'

'Because it's an exhibition of my work. Not his.'
Tiah struggled for patience, for understanding, her
efforts very nearly negated as Claudia objected
calmly,

'But his work has always been so much better.
You wouldn't have known which end of a paintbrush
to hold if he hadn't shown you. Oliver always said
you hadn't a grain of real talent, but you were to
be encouraged because your watercolours made a
nice little hobby. Darling—I don't want to be
unkind, but you understand that, I know you do.
And surely there was room for just one of his real
works of art among all that stuff of yours?'

Claudia was behaving as if she had no inkling of
how these things were done. But she wasn't an
idiot and must be aware that other people's work,
no matter how good, couldn't be planted, willy-
nilly, in an exhibition of work by one named artist.

The denigrating words regarding her own work didn't hurt. Lucas believed in her and had taught her to believe in herself. And perhaps Oliver hadn't been the great artist that he and Claudia had always maintained he was.

Tiah took a deep breath, her eyes on the road ahead. Somehow she had to get through to Claudia, no matter how brutal it made her seem. 'You're not a fool, so please don't talk like one——'

But Claudia wasn't listening, and her voice as it cut across Tiah's was soft and dreamy.

'We had such a lovely time in the park. I used to take him there when he was just a little boy. And this morning was such fun—it's a pity you had to miss it. We went to all his favourite haunts—the playground first, of course! He does so love the swings, though he will go so high! And I'm always afraid he'll tumble off and hurt himself. I can't help worrying about him. I know I shouldn't, but he's all I have. Then we went round to the lake to feed the ducks. Did you know——' her bright, glittering eyes turned to Tiah, 'there's a pair of swans there now. We were both so thrilled! What a pity you weren't there with us, dear!'

The dreamy voice filled the car, making Tiah's mouth go dry, her stomach clench with dread. Claudia was no longer using the past tense, reliving old memories. She was talking as though Oliver had been with her that morning, a laughing child again, enjoying an outing with his elder sister, the two of them happy in a world that didn't exist because one of them was dead and long gone.

CHAPTER EIGHT

THERE was a chill in the late afternoon air that penetrated Tiah's anorak and she shivered as she walked quickly down the incline to the bridge. But the coldness came more from within her than from the cool October air.

She leaned wearily against the stone parapet, watching the dark rush of water beneath. Tomorrow was her twenty-third birthday and since that awful conversation in the car, driving home from Compton, Claudia had been bright and cheerful, throwing herself into the preparations for tomorrow night's dinner party.

Tiah found it impossible to reconcile the patently normal behaviour with that of the woman who had spoken so irrationally the other day.

If only Claudia would admit to herself that her beloved younger brother was gone beyond recall!

The whispering had been the first sign that anything was wrong. And when it had started, a few weeks after Oliver's death, Tiah had spoken to their doctor—a kindly, dedicated soul who knew the family well. He had done his best to allay her fears over Claudia's state of mind. 'Give it time,' he had said. 'She'll work it out for herself in time. Basically, she's a sensible woman, and grief affects us all in different ways. Once she allows herself to grieve openly, to go through the terrible trauma of admitting a loved one is gone, she'll be fine.'

Platitudes that had seemed to make good sense at the time, had reassured, helping Tiah to be patient. But the things he had said held no validity now because something in Claudia would never let go. Oliver's dying words had bound her, too.

Unless—Tiah's brow furrowed as her fingers picked at the lichened stone beneath her hands— unless Polly had been right?

Had Claudia, with some warped reasoning of her own, been trying to make Tiah believe that Oliver was still near, loving them, that they were still a close-knit family unit, a unit Tiah must not break? Tiah could not go, find her independence, if she were made to believe that Oliver was still there.

And Claudia's behaviour had grown so much worse since Lucas had appeared on the scene. Claudia had not wanted anyone from the outside to destroy their little world. She had seen Lucas as a threat and had instinctively reacted to that threat in the way she knew would worry Tiah the most.

But even if that were the case, it didn't mean that Claudia was not sick. Tiah's responsibility would be in no way diminished.

She could deny her love for Lucas, the love that was driving her strongly to relegate the past to where it belonged. Yes, she could deny that love, stay here, try to forget Lucas, resume the old quiet pattern of her days, care for Claudia because she was owed . . .

And day after day the stream would flow on beneath the bridge, disappearing in the long shadows. And she would watch the ripples as she was watching them now, ever changing yet constant, until she grew old . . .

And suddenly she knew there had to be more than that. More for herself and for Lucas. Her logical mind at last accepted the fact that a marriage such as she had had with Oliver couldn't happen again. The past, whatever it had held, was over and done with.

She wanted to marry Lucas, to be made whole by him, bear his children, grow old with him and not her memories. And she had to trust her instincts now, because they were all she had.

She turned to the house, the cold wind whipping the hair across her face as she moved quickly towards the building. It was a lovely, graceful place, but with an air of melancholia, sinister, even, sometimes, when the light was fading from the sky, the dark trees and high black scudding clouds emphasising its isolation.

Her breath came shallowly. She had to speak to Lucas. Now. Tell him she would marry him, if he still wanted it—and after what had happened at the exhibition he might have changed his mind. But she had to find out, and find out now, before tomorrow, because tomorrow could be too late. Whatever lay behind Claudia's invitation boded no good. No good at all.

The large hall was deathly silent, its darkness illuminated feebly by a single table-lamp, casting high dark shadows which fell across Oliver's self-portraits but somehow, eerily, emphasising the painted dead eyes.

Her fingers shook as she dialled, praying for Lucas to be home. She needed to hear his voice. The presence of Oliver was deadly, oppressive, as if he were waiting, watching over the woman he had loved, as if he knew she was looking for happiness in another man's arms, betraying him and the love he had for her.

Tiah took a deep gulp of air, steadying herself, the untypical nervous fears brought about by Claudia's behaviour forgotten, as Lucas's voice reached out and seemed to touch her, enfolding her in his warmth, his love.

'I was about to phone you, sweetheart,'

She closed her eyes, drowning in her love for him, her gratitude for his love for her, and he told her, his voice slightly mocking.

'Your exhibition's got off to a good start. Three of your paintings already sport nice little red stickers—and no quibbling about the price, apparently. Or aren't you interested in filthy lucre!'

'No. Yes—well——' she laughed weakly, confused, longing for the feel of his arms around her, the seductive touch of his lips on hers. 'I've had other things on my mind. Lucas——' her voice faltered, then firmed. 'Lucas, is your offer of marriage still open?'

She felt the tautness of his sudden silence, could almost see the wary expression in his eyes.

'It depends on who's applying.'

'I am,' she answered quickly, jerkily, hearing his softly breathed,

'Do you mean that, Tiah?'

'I mean it. I most certainly mean it.' A convulsive movement in her diaphragm made her breathless, her voice husky, and he said urgently,

'I'm coming over, love. Or better still, get yourself here. Fast. I want to plant my seal of ownership on you, make good and sure you don't change your mind.' There was raw emotion in his deep voice and she knew what he meant, knew what he wanted. And she wanted it too, he didn't know how much. But there were things she had to do here.

'I can't,' she told him shakily, wishing with all her heart that she could just go to him, never look back. 'But I'll be seeing you tomorrow evening.'

'That long?' He sounded flat, and added warily, 'Okay, have it your way. You're worth waiting for. And to tell you the truth I'd actually steeled myself to wait a whole lot longer for you to pull your head out of the sand and realise that you wanted me around for the rest of your life. I love you, Tiah.'

'I know.' Both hands cradled the receiver, as if that physical pressure could actually bring him closer. 'I know.'

She stared at the buzzing instrument long after Lucas had hung up, then replaced it, regretfully. A feeling of absolute aloneness settled on her like a heavy damp pall, but she squared her shoulders and went to look for Claudia.

'Of course everything will be all right tomorrow evening.' Claudia laid down her embroidery and turned bewildered eyes on Tiah. 'It's your birthday celebration—not a large dinner party, of course— but a pleasant one, I hope. So why shouldn't everything be all right?'

Tiah couldn't bring herself to answer that. Cowardly, maybe, but there it was. How could she say, to this calm, entirely rational woman, the woman who had taken the place of the mother she had never known, the sister she had never had, 'Because you might just pull something crazy out of that bag of tricks of yours'?

She couldn't do that. If things were indeed going to be all right then a remark such as that would more or less guarantee that they would be all wrong! She wandered the room, uneasy, touching things, her voice tight despite the effort she made to make it otherwise,

'I just thought it strange that you should invite Lucas along. At one time you seemed pretty antagonistic to the idea of my seeing him.'

'Oh, hardly *antagonistic*, dear.' The white head shook a gentle denial. 'On closer acquaintance I find him a charming, harmless young man.'

Harmless! Tiah almost choked. It wasn't a harmless man who had cut straight through her painstakingly erected defences, shredding them so that they became nothing, worse than useless, bending her will to match his own. Oh no, Lucas Clent was far from harmless!

'Why don't you sit down, dear, and stop pacing.' Claudia stabbed her needle into the fabric she was working on and got fluidly to her feet. 'I'll bring something cold in on a tray. We can eat in here for once. Polly and I have been so busy preparing for tomorrow evening that we didn't give a thought to tonight's meal.' Her smile was kind, the look in her eyes concerned. 'Do sit down by the fire. You've been out all day—no wonder you're tired and edgy.'

She crossed to where the drinks were and poured sherry into a delicate crystal glass, putting it in Tiah's hands.

'If you won't look after yourself properly, then I must do it for you. And don't worry, everything's going to be all right.'

The words were meant to be reassuring, but as Claudia left the room Tiah thought they sounded more like a threat.

And even as she dressed for dinner the next evening Tiah wasn't at all sure that, as Claudia had promised, everything was going to be all right. She was picking up undercurrents, or thought she was. But maybe it was all in her mind and she was in danger of becoming as crazy as poor Claudia was at times.

That morning Claudia had told her to keep out of the way. The old 'uns, she had stated—referring to herself and Polly—would do all the work for a change. It was her birthday, so why didn't she take herself to Compton? Have her hair done, perhaps, treat herself to a leisurely lunch?

The suggestion had been tempting. She didn't need a hair-do, she always managed it herself, but she could go and see her own exhibition at last, discover which paintings had sold—Lucas hadn't said. Call in on him at the *Gazette* offices, take him to lunch. See him. Talk to him. Plan their future. *She needed him.*

But something had kept her here. Despite her fondness of Claudia, she couldn't trust her. So she had spent the day tidying the garden, cutting away perennial foliage that had been blackened by the first frost, barrowing it away for Joe to burn when he came next weekend. And while she had been snatching a cup of coffee in the kitchen Polly had told her, 'She's really gone to town for tonight. I'm not telling you what she's giving you to eat— she'd flay me alive—but she's been getting everything just so. Flowers for the table, the best china and glass. And she's had me polishing silver until I thought me fingers would drop off! It's going to be soft lights and sweet music and cham— Oops!' Polly clapped a large red hand over her mouth, her black eyes popping. 'Me and me wagging tongue! Get back to your digging, or whatever, before I spill the lot!'

So it seemed all right, but Tiah couldn't be sure. Staring at her reflection in the mirror she felt tense and shivery, not at all in a party mood. But that could be due to anticipation. Seeing Lucas for the first time since she had agreed to marry him, the strain of getting through this evening with Claudia present—when she and Lucas would want to be alone, to make love, make plans, make love . . .

Colour flooded her face, heightening the brilliance of her eyes. That was her trouble, she pinpointed, glad to find a rational explanation. Plain, old-fashioned frustration!

Tonight she had left her hair loose, but caught back from either side of her face with jade combs, emphasising the pure lines of her facial bone structure, the slender sweep of her throat. Her dress was jade, too, a silk chiffon that brushed her calves, the draped cross-over bodice revealing a deep V of ivory-tinted skin. And her long ear-droppers were brilliantly cut, tiny emeralds. Claudia had produced them this morning, as a surprise gift since Tiah had known about the suit, having chosen the fabric and stood about for fittings. The emeralds had belonged to Claudia's mother and the gesture had touched Tiah deeply, reinforcing her fondness for the woman who had been so good to her . . .

It was almost half past seven and Tiah wanted to be the first to meet Lucas when he arrived, to have just a little time alone with him. She didn't want him to tell Claudia about their wedding plans, not just yet. Acceptance would have to be won gradually. To break the news too suddenly, too abruptly, could send Claudia slipping back into that dark pit of unbalance that was so worrying.

Passing Claudia's room she could hear sounds of her moving about, the closing of the heavy wardrobe door, and Tiah ran, suddenly light-hearted, down the stairs. A beautiful woman waiting for the man she loved. No more, no less. No uneasy undercurrents, nothing for this moment but this delightful, soaring anticipation.

Standing in the open doorway, shivering a little as the night air touched her, she saw his car's raking headlights before she heard the sound of the engine and she slipped out of the sheltering doorway and, heedless of the way the slender heels of her strappy shoes twisted beneath her, ran to meet him.

She met him on the bridge, and his headlight must have picked her out because he was already braking, had the passenger door open for her as she slipped between the car and the parapet on the bridge. The door closed with a soft clunk, extinguishing the courtesy light, the warm darkness cocooning them, isolating them. And she was in his arms, held close, feeling his warmth, the beat of his heart beneath her hand as she slipped it under his jacket, resting her palm against the smooth white silk of his shirt. And his mouth was hot and urgent, covering her own, plundering its willing sweetness, and he whispered huskily against her mouth,

'Are you entirely sure of this, Tiah? I couldn't stand it if you weren't, if you changed your mind,' and she gently nipped his lower lip between her small white teeth, feeling the play of her smile produce an answering one for him as she murmured,

'Entirely, completely, utterly sure.'

He shifted, moving closer in the limited space, and her body quivered as his arms engulfed her, his one hand tangled in her hair, holding her head to suit his needs exactly, his other hand slipping unerringly inside the V of her bodice, easing the fabric aside as he took one aroused breast in the cupping palm of his hand, his thumb moving with exquisite enticement over her rosy, hardened nipple.

Tiah clung helplessly to him, a slow deep ache filling her lower body, and she felt the answering arousal in him and wished they could stay like this for ever, but he moved away from her, his deep voice not quite steady as he told her,

'Any more of this and I'm not going to be able to stop myself from taking you right here, my love. And an encounter of that kind, in the front seats of a car, is not what I have in mind for us. For us, it's going to be perfect. Besides,' his teeth glinted whitely in the darkness, 'Claudia will be sending out a search party! Have you broken our news to her?'

He sounded supremely confident, supremely happy, as he pushed back his tumbled hair—the soft unruly lock that had a habit of falling over his forehead—reaching for the ignition key, and she told him, her hand covering his just briefly,

'No, I haven't told her yet. We'll keep it to ourselves a while longer.' She sounded slightly breathless, her body aching for his still. 'I'll break it to her gently, some other time. Let's leave it for this evening.'

'Why? Ashamed of me?' He slewed round to face her squarely, and although the interior of the car was dark she could see the taut lines of his face. 'Or just letting things ride in case you might want to change your mind?'

'Please trust me,' she answered softly, sadly,

catching his hand between hers and dropping her bright head to place a moist kiss on its palm. 'Trust me. I won't change my mind. It's just——' Wide eyes pleaded, needing his understanding. 'Claudia has grown to rely on my company. She hates the thought of living alone. And I'll be leaving——'

'Too right you will.' He started the car, racing the engine, his mouth grim. 'Too damn right you'll be leaving!'

It took only seconds to reach the house but Tiah had managed to straighten her clothing, her hair, and Lucas had forgotten his sudden surge of temper, or a least subdued it, and was urbane, superbly at ease as he walked behind Tiah into the hall, lifting his head to smile up at Claudia as she drifted down the stairs in pleated violet silk.

'I thought I heard a car,' her smile was unalloyed welcome and Lucas produced a posy of freesias, 'For you, Claudia,' and to Tiah, 'I guess I shall have to give you your birthday gift some other time.' And from the way he said that, the sudden closed expression in his eyes, the slight, involuntary movement of his hand towards the breast pocket of his immaculately cut dark suit, she guessed his gift for her had been a ring.

Tears of regret choked her throat. What must he be thinking of her! A grown woman—already once married—too bashful and nervous to break the news of her engagement to the woman who was like a mother to her! He must think her a fool! Or devious.

But she would explain it all to him. One day, when they had time. And she pushed the brief miserable mood aside, determined to show him by look and gesture that he was her man, and having recognised that, capitulated, nothing on earth would make her change her mind.

And if Claudia didn't notice the way she looked at him, the way their eyes held and clung, then she must be blind. She must be picking up the vibrations right now, Tiah thought, the champagne they had had with the superb meal making her feel light-headed, optimistic. And with the seeds already planted Tiah could break the news, gently, quite soon. In a day or two. Tomorrow, even.

Claudia would be all right and would get used to living on her own. She was a survivor. Polly would keep an eye on her, keep her company. And she and Lucas would spend much of their time in this area, he had told her that much, and they would be able to visit often. And to look at Claudia now, poised, the perfect hostess, no one would believe that only a few days ago she had been talking as though Oliver were still alive, a little boy playing in the park again.

She cradled her brandy glass in her hands, her eyes meeting his, darkened now to indigo in the mellow candlelight. His eyes held messages that turned her bones to water, and she could have hit herself for imagining that this evening could be a disaster.

Everything had been perfect. The meal, the wine, the conversation. The room was small, intimate. Lots of Oliver's paintings around, that went without saying. His photographs, too. But in the candlelight they were scarcely noticeable, certainly not intrusive. And the sound from the tape deck was pleasing—something classical, slow and dreamy, and Lucas was telling Claudia about life in the States, and she was asking intelligent questions, her dark eyes intent on his face.

And then the music suddenly changed. The terrible, spine-chilling strains of *Danse Macabre* blaring out, filling the room until the air was thick with it, and Tiah sucked in her breath, her heart thumping until she thought it would choke her.

She shot an anguished look at Claudia and knew she had planned this, making sure that Tiah was forcibly reminded, by Oliver's favourite music, of his unrelinquished rights.

It had been done quite deliberately. And how the woman who had come to mean so much to her could do such a sick, sly thing, Tiah couldn't begin to fathom. And the malevolent gloating look in those dark eyes brought nausea rising in Tiah's throat.

Whatever else she deserved, she didn't deserve this. And she should have confided in Lucas, weeks ago, told him of Claudia's sickness. Instead, she had said nothing, for Claudia's sake, believing that she, Tiah, could handle it as she had handled it before. But the sickness was obviously increasing and the thing that Tiah had always fought—the idea of Claudia being shut away in a home—now seemed a dreadful possibility.

Rising hastily, pushing her chair back clumsily, intent on leaving the room before she disgraced herself, she headed for the door, closing it on Claudia's soft, apologetic words,

'I'm so sorry, Lucas. I had no idea that piece of music was on the end of that tape. It was Oliver's favourite, he was always playing it. We used to call it his "theme song". It's so sad, isn't it, the way it always upsets poor Tiah? You have to understand— it reminds her of the only man she's ever loved.'

CHAPTER NINE

'WE have to talk.'

His mouth was grim, lines of strain etched deeply on his darkly handsome face, and Tiah, pale-faced but recovered from her violent bout of retching, watched him warily from the open doorway.

He was standing with his back to the open fire; the debris of the meal on the candlelit table looked squalid now. There was no sign of Claudia; Tiah moistened her lips and Lucas commanded, 'Get a coat. You're coming with me.'

'I'm what?' She didn't understand. She had expected his anger—after the insinuations Claudia had made. It was Claudia's duplicity, the horrible evidence of her increasing illness, that had upset her so, not the music in itself, but he didn't know that, and she couldn't bring herself to tell him, to explain, not here, not now. And she could have coped with his anger. Somehow. But this iciness, this total unremitting hardness—no way!

'You are coming with me. To my flat. You will be staying overnight so bring a toothbrush. We need to talk, and we can't do it here.' He enunciated the words coldly, extremely carefully, as if he were talking to a retarded child—a particularly irritating one—and she shook her head in miserable negation.

'I can't.'

'You can and you will. Even if I have to drag you there. I'm getting you out of this mausoleum—at least until I'm satisfied that we've reached some definite understanding, one way or the other. Claudia knows you're coming with me. I've told her,' he added bitingly, and her eyes widened incredulously.

'Claudia didn't—didn't mind?'

'Why should she?'

He advanced towards her, and she flattened herself against the door jamb, sensing the barely controlled violence in him, the hardness of his eyes making her feel desperately alone, alone and terrified that she had lost him.

'We are living in the nineteen eighties,' he snapped out curtly. 'Or hadn't you noticed? You're not a quivering virgin, just out of the schoolroom—you're a grown woman with one marriage behind you already. And judging by your response to me, it was a highly physical one.'

His hand gripped her shoulders, his hard fingers biting into her flesh. There was no tenderness there, none of the gentleness she had learned to expect from him, as he propelled her into the dimly lit hall.

'Get your things. We are going to talk, away from here, and don't look as if you're afraid I'll rape you. I won't touch you. I don't think I even want to touch you. Get!'

She got. Fetched a coat, the first thing she came across in the hall cupboard, forgot about a toothbrush, comb, anything else, mesmerised by the cold calmness in him, by the strange feeling of foreboding.

Why hadn't Claudia raised a single objection when Lucas had told her of his intention of taking her back with him? Claudia would go to any lengths to ruin their relationship. Tiah had, at last, accepted that when Oliver's 'theme song' had blared out over the dinner-table. So what was going on in her poor sick mind now?

It was a question she was unable to answer, but it stayed with her during the journey to Lucas's flat, keeping her silent, although he wasn't saying anything, either. He seemed alien to her, the man she had grown to love hidden away in the cold shell of a stranger.

The charged atmosphere remained, thickened, as he took her up in the private lift and ushered her into the sitting-room.

'Make yourself comfortable. I'll get some coffee.'

And when he came back with the tray he had removed his jacket, his tie. The superbly cut silk shirt clung to his masculine body, the narrow dark trousers clinging to the lines of his long legs, clipping his neat buttocks. And Tiah wept inside for love of him, hunching herself up in a corner of the sofa because she wanted to make herself small, unseen, not here, anywhere away from the mess she had made of something that could have been superb.

He poured the coffee, his back to her, still rigidly controlled, outwardly calm. Cold. And as she took the drink he offered the cup rattled wildly on the saucer and he frowned impatiently, taking it from her shaking hands and putting it within reach on a side table.

'So why did you say you'd marry me, Tiah?'

He swung a chair round, straddled it, and sat facing her, his eyes icily derisive. And she couldn't answer him, her throat was too tight with tension, her mind too tired—like a wild thing, caged and terrified, too exhausted from battering against unyielding bars to be able to find any words, let alone the right ones.

But he persisted, his mouth tight, savage. 'It's a question I've been asking myself over the last two hours. I need to know, and only you can tell me.'

'Because I wanted to,' she answered chokily, at last.

'Past tense,' he noted, a wry twist to his mouth. 'You wanted to escape the prison you'd put yourself in, is that it? It is, isn't it, Tiah?' he ground out when she didn't reply. 'Okay, so you can't talk about it. I figured that much.'

His voice grated, the only indication of his stress, and Tiah frantically twisted the filmy fabric of her skirts between her fingers, her pain unbearable and only partly controlled. If she lost that control now she would break down utterly, tell him everything, and this she could not do. She had nothing left but her pride, and it was the only thing she had to cling to.

'Still not saying anything?'

He sounded as if he hated her, and she lifted her head to stare at him mutinously, her eyes dropping away again as she met the bitterness in his. He took a deep breath and rubbed his hands over his eyes tiredly. 'So I'll do the talking. Stop me if there's anything you want to add or subtract. You wanted escape and took me as a lifeline. I don't blame you for that—I'm strong enough to take the strain. I love you, you know that, and I can turn you on, you know that, too. But when it came to the crunch you couldn't turn your back on the past, could you? You wouldn't tell Claudia that we were to be married—that would have made it seem real, wouldn't it? You ran from the room, in obvious distress, when a piece of music reminded you of Oliver. You won't discuss your marriage to him with me, you turn your home into a shrine to his memory, you even tried to get one of his paintings hung with your own. You wept when you looked at that drawing you'd made of him. You can't let him go, won't go forward. I'm willing to help you, I'll always love you, but I can't and I won't fight a ghost.'

She looked at him numbly. 'It's not like that.'

'Then what the hell is it like?' He jerked up from the chair, his movements sharp, and he raked his hands through his hair, swinging round to face her, hard eyes impaling her. *'Tell me, dammit?'*

She couldn't. She had left it far too late.

If she had done what her innate fastidiousness had prevented her from doing—explained poor Claudia's precarious mental state—weeks, months ago, then this gross misinterpretation of his would never have occurred. She had been trying to protect Claudia and it was too late now. Laying the blame for all the misunderstandings at Claudia's feet would only seem to him like the juvenile wrigglings of a cowardly mind.

Each time Lucas had seen Claudia she had appeared perfectly rational, perfectly sane. While she, herself, must have seemed quite the opposite!

He came to sit beside her, taking the hands which seemed in danger of destroying the dress she wore, in both of his. And if she hadn't known better, hadn't felt the birth of something akin to hatred coming from him, she would have said that the glittering sapphire brilliance of his eyes was caused by a film of tears.

Her own inner tears had solidified in a painful lump in her chest, making it difficult to speak, to breathe. But she managed huskily, the steady warmth of his hands giving her courage, 'I want to be your wife. Trust me, please. That's if you still want me,' she added uncertainly, hearing his harshly indrawn breath, her body going cold as he immediately removed his hands from hers and slumped forwards, his elbows on his knees, his dark head resting against clenched fists.

'Trust you?' he said at last, raising his head to look at her from tired eyes. 'I suppose I shall have to. God knows, I still want you, love you.'

There were tiny lines of weariness spreading out from eyes which were slightly red-rimmed, over-bright, and she closed her own, hating herself for bringing him this grief, and he got to his feet and she watched him walk across the floor, her heart twisting inside her.

Moments later he came back, a tiny box and an official-looking sheet of paper in his hands, and he slumped heavily back down beside her, not touching her.

'Let's see how far we get, shall we?'

The ring he put on her finger was a perfect sapphire, mounted in heavy wrought gold, fitting beautifully, and he told her, his voice roughened, 'I guessed the size. You have slim fingers, Tiah. They said they'd alter it if it didn't fit. And that——' he dropped the paper on to the side table, next to her untouched coffee, 'that is a special licence.'

Her eyes winged to his, questioning, and her heart pattered on, picked up speed as he explained, 'I have to go to New York on Sunday evening. I've known for a couple of days—something urgent has cropped up. And roughly five minutes after I'd agreed to more or less drop everything here and fly out a month earlier than I'd originally intended, you dropped your bombshell. Said you'd marry me. I wanted to give you the ring this evening, make plans—but you weren't willing apparently—you wanted to keep everything under wraps. I'd hoped you'd agree to get married straight away, on Saturday, hence the special licence. I wanted you to come to the States with me, as my wife. I made the arrangements but fully conceded that you might prefer to wait and do the thing with more dignity and less haste when I got back—around Christmas. But I've changed my mind about giving you that choice.'

He took her chin with a hand that felt like steel, turning her head, forcing his gaze on hers, pinning her down.

'After what happened this evening I won't take the risk of leaving you here, shut up with your precious memories of Oliver. If you really want to marry me, you'll agree to a wedding on Saturday, fly to New York with me on Sunday. It's your choice, Tiah.'

It was her choice and she had to take it. Suddenly, her eyes filled with the tears she had held back for so long and she whispered, 'Yes, Lucas. Saturday,' and his fingers brushed away the spilling tears, his sigh deep and ragged as he got quickly to his feet.

She heard the clink of the brandy decanter against glass. He poured two large measures and handed her one.

'You look bushed. Drink this, then we'll get to bed. And tomorrow morning I'll take you back to Deepdene and you can break the news to Claudia, get her organised for Saturday morning. I expect she'll want to be at the wedding,' he put in drily, noting her blank expression.

Would she hell! Tiah thought inelegantly, sipping quickly at the mellow warming liquid to prevent herself from giving any more away.

Claudia had done her best—or worst—to ruin any chance she had of a deep and lasting relationship with Lucas. She would not want to dance at their wedding!

'And your mother, will she be there?'

'No way!'

The vehemence of his reply caught her off guard and her eyes winged open, bewildered.

'What she knows about happy marriages could be engraved on a pin head. She'd be a Jonah,' he told her harshly.

'But she is your mother,' Tiah objected. She privately regarded Ellie as a vain, self-absorbed creature, only seeing things the way she thought she should be able to see them, not as they really were. But if Lucas could forgive her rejection of the child that he had been—then it could only benefit both him and his mother. Rancour such as his could only corrode the unforgiver more than the unforgiven. But he shrugged, draining his glass and setting it back on the table with a no-nonsense click.

'So? We're not talking about Ellie. We're making arrangements for our wedding. I'll leave you at Deepdene tomorrow morning.' His mouth tightened as if he found the concept distasteful. 'I've got urgent business to get through at the *Gazette* before I go to New York. But I'll drive over tomorrow evening and pick you up. You'll spend the night here again. Unconventional, I know, but I need to be sure that your late husband's mementoes won't change your mind.'

'They won't,' she stated as calmly as she could. He had been desperately hurt over what had happened, what he believed had happened, so she couldn't entirely blame him for speaking of Oliver so bitterly.

She finished what was left of her brandy and stood up, feeling oddly shaky, drained. 'I'd like to sleep now.'

He ignored that, for the moment, his face set, pale beneath his lingering summer tan.

'Does Claudia drive?'

'Of course.' His question puzzled her, she wasn't thinking straight, and when he added, 'Good, she can get herself and whoever else you want to invite over to Compton in time for the wedding,' she had to shake her head to clear it. Claudia wouldn't be there to see her married to Lucas, she was very sure of that.

'Just pack whatever you want to be married in,' Lucas was telling her. 'And something to travel in the next day. You can buy whatever else you need in New York.'

'Of course.' He was talking as though their marriage was to be a business merger, a boring one at that. And although it made her want to cry again, because they seemed to have lost something infinitely precious, she couldn't blame him.

He couldn't trust her yet, not totally. He believed she was still in love with Oliver. She knew only time could teach him to trust her completely. She didn't doubt his love, or hers, and that, for the moment, was something she had to hold on to. And it was enough. It had to be.

He showed her to one of the bathrooms. Clinical,

bare of anything of his. So he must use the other, she thought tiredly, leaning her hot forehead against the cool pale grey tiles. He had given her a clean pair of his pyjamas, and she found a toothbrush, still in its cellophane wrapper, on the smoked glass shelf above the navy blue washbasin.

She showered quickly, the needles of hot water going some way to soothing her wound-up inner tension, and she put the pyjamas on, struggling to roll up the much too long sleeves and legs, almost too tired to do that.

The softly carpeted corridor was silent as she padded along it to the door he had indicated as he had shown her to the bathroom. It was the spare, he had told her without a trace of feeling in his voice. She hadn't thought it possible that they could share his flat, practically on the eve of their wedding, and not share a bed. She craved the reassurance of his arms.

He had wanted her earlier this evening—it seemed a lifetime ago—when she had slipped into his car as he had arrived. There had been no mistaking the extent of his arousal. And he could arouse her, too, make her feel gloriously, shamelessly wanton, and they loved each other, and separate rooms were a sad indication of the edgy, watchful state of their relationship.

Fumbling a little, she opened the bedroom door, blinking owlishly because after the emotional turmoil of the evening she could hardly keep her eyes open. Then her heart lurched, missing a beat, racing on again, because he was standing there, so perhaps he did want to love her, hold her, after all. Perhaps he had put the pain of the evening's events behind him, along with her far from satisfying answers to his probing questions.

'Don't look so shattered,' he told her roughly. 'I've only been making your bed up. I don't intend to share it. We're both too uptight to gain anything from an experience which should be mind-blowingly beautiful. Besides,' he added savagely, 'the way I'm feeling right now would guarantee a most unfavourable comparison with that superb lover, your late lamented husband. And all the signals I've been getting indicate that he was just that.'

The deliberate cruelty of his parting shot tormented her, and she crept miserably beneath the duvet, getting tangled up in his too-big pyjamas. She sniffed dejectedly into the lavender-scented pillow and hoped and prayed that their marriage would not be conducted on these lines of verbal sniping, that he would not continually compare himself with Oliver, or ask her to.

This was a new and dismaying departure for the man she had always looked on as being superbly confident, sure of what he was and who he was. The idea that she, who loved him, should be the one to make him prey to tormenting self-doubt was abhorrent to her, and it stuck in her mind, keeping sleep at a distance, because she didn't know what she could do about it.

But when they had been married for a little while she would be able, at last, to explain about Claudia. By then he would have grown to trust her love for him. If she told him now he wouldn't believe her.

Eventually she slept, fitfully, only to be woken by the sound of the bedroom door swinging open, and she propped herself on one elbow, fumbling for the bedside light, and Lucas said throatily, 'It's only me. I can't sleep without you. Move over, Tiah.'

He didn't wait for her to do that, but slid in beside her, beneath the duvet, his strong naked arms gathering her to him, his hands curving softly around her breasts.

'I want to sleep with you. Just sleep, God, I'm tired,' he murmured blearily. 'I only want to hold you close.'

His arms cradled her, their relaxed weight heavy, the comforting pressure of his languid hands on her breasts deeply and satisfyingly erotic. Amazingly, he was already falling asleep and Tiah, too, relaxed, fitting herself into the curve of his body, the feeling good, so good . . .

She woke, hazily coming to life, his dark head close to hers on the pillow, his arm heavy across her body. Love for him curled lazily inside her, sweet and languorous, and she brushed a kiss against his slightly parted lips—softer, so much more vulnerable in sleep—and saw the sooty curves of his lashes drift open, move, revealing sleepy slits of deepest sapphire.

'Tiah?' The eyes widened, hazing over with a need that was betrayed by the sudden, erratic beating of a pulse in the hollow of his throat.

'I think it's late. We've overslept,' she told him unsteadily, assailed by the sharp spear of desire that stabbed remorselessly through her, her fingers fluttering uncertainly to touch his face, feeling the roughness of stubble on his jawline.

'Late?' he echoed huskily. 'I suppose it could be.' His eyes dropped to the gaping jacket top of her borrowed pyjamas and his hand moved, his index finger stroking gently down her throat, following the curve of her breasts until he found the hardening peaks. Then, slowly, his lips continued the sensual exploration and Tiah arched against him, her need spiralling beyond control, her body slicked with beads of perspiration.

At the husky, almost feral sound she produced in her throat he lifted his head and gave her a long, complicated look.

'This is no time to start anything.' He rolled away from her, flicking on the bedside light, lifting the wrist that bore his watch, and Tiah shuddered with the chilling effects of rejection. 'You were right, it's almost ten,' he groaned. 'We've got one hell of a load to get through before the ceremony tomorrow.'

At his words a flick of excitement zipped through her, banishing frustration. Tomorrow was their wedding day. And she scrambled out of bed as he threw back the duvet and loped across the room to pull back the heavy curtains that had kept out the morning light.

Not that there was much of that, she thought, her eyes dwelling on the sleek panther-like elegance of him as he stretched, his naked torso displaying the fluid strength of perfectly conditioned muscle and bone, the pyjama bottoms he wore hanging low on his narrow hips.

The rain, falling steadily from a pewter grey sky, slashed against the windows, the pattern of sound emphasising their cocoon of warm intimacy, and her throat tightened because she only had to look at him to want him and he, obviously, had other things on his mind.

He turned, pushing long supple fingers through his rumpled hair, grinning at her, his lazily amused eyes sweeping over her.

'Waif!'

The small tension eased, physical desire receding

to a bearable level beneath his amusement. She must look like something left over from a jumble sale, she conceded, her silvery eyes lighting in a smile as he told her, 'Get a move on, sweetheart. Breakfast first, then I'll run you back to Deepdene.'

'Have you time?' She was running the fingers of one hand through her own mussed hair, her other hand clutching at the bunched-up waistband of his pyjamas, and he slapped her bottom lightly.

'Get moving, there's time for everything.'

But not for making love, she thought drearily as she tugged off his pyjamas and dropped them in the linen basket of the bathroom she had used the night before. But perhaps he had been right to call a halt. Neither of them would want to rush their first complete act of lovemaking together. His sudden withdrawal did not have to mean that he was afraid of the comparisons she might make between him and Oliver.

Determinedly talking herself out of her dejected mood, she washed quickly, brushed her teeth, conscious of the passage of time. They both had a great deal to do today. Breaking the news to Claudia would not be easy. She definitely wasn't looking forward to that, but it had to be done. And she would need to speak privately to Polly, ask her to keep an eye on Claudia, to get in touch with the doctor if she seemed to be taking what she would see as Tiah's defection too badly.

Without any enthusiasm she got into the dress she had worn the night before, surveying her mirrored image with acute distaste. Devoid of make-up, her face looked strangely childlike, and the dress, so pretty and flattering in candlelight, looked tawdry in the grey light of a wet October morning. Her hair was a tangled mane, and she

couldn't find a comb. Grimacing at herself, she
turned away from the mirror. There was nothing
she could do about the way she looked.

But tomorrow she and Lucas would be married
and the past would belong in the past, and could
stay there. A sudden, winging surge of happiness
suffused her, and she followed her nose to the
kitchen, her misgivings over Claudia, her distaste
for the way she looked, forgotten.

'I could get a taxi back,' she told him from the
open kitchen doorway.

He was dressed in the trousers of a dark lovat
suit and a light fawn shirt, tailored to his body—a
tall lean devil with incredible sapphire eyes and
soft, nearly black hair. And she loved him. *Oh
God, how she loved him!*

'No need. I can take you.' He basted sizzling
eggs in a pan, glancing at her wickedly. 'Just think
how your reputation would suffer—hiring a cabbie
at this time of day to drive you home in your party
finery!'

Tiah made toast and poured coffee while Lucas
dealt with the eggs and bacon and the atmosphere
was serene, untroubled, as if they had been friends
for years—not almost lovers. As if they had been
married for years—and not about to take their
vows tomorrow. And she said, as they sat down to
eat, 'Why don't I drive myself back here later this
afternoon? I could arrange for Joe to return the
car to Claudia, and it would save you having to
fetch me. You said you'd be busy today.'

He was buttering a slice of toast, his strong
fingers deft, and he looked up at her, his eyes
blank, but surely not suspecting the real reason
behind that suggestion. She didn't want to hang.
around at Deepdene any longer than necessary,

with the shade of Oliver an insistent reminder of what Claudia would be bound to see as her betrayal. She wanted nothing sad or distressing to mar her happy anticipation of tomorrow.

'It sounds like a good idea,' he said cagily, then smiled, relaxed. 'Okay, I'll give you a spare key. With not having to take time out to fetch you, I should be back here around seven.' His eyes crinkled at the corners. 'There's steak in the fridge if you feel like cooking. And if you can find time between making our meal and making yourself beautiful for me, poke around and see whether you'd prefer the study or the spare bedroom for your studio.'

He swallowed the last of his coffee and stood up from the table, laughter in his eyes as he looked down at her. 'I shall expect you to follow your own career—you're too talented to give it up. But I hope you noted my order of priorities!' and she thrust her nose in the air and said huffily,

'I always said you were the last of the chauvinists!' but inside she was melting because her future was Lucas and nothing else mattered now.

The underlying thread of anticipation, the sharp sexual awareness that was never far beneath the surface, his brand of light amusing conversation which, she guessed, was calculated to keep her at her ease, combined to guarantee that the time spent driving back to Deepdene was free from the anxieties that had beset her earlier.

But, as he braked in front of the house and told her, 'We'll go and break the good news to Claudia,' Tiah stiffened. Staring straight ahead, her eyes fixed on the elegant lines of the house, she said hurriedly, 'Give me five minutes with her, Lucas.'

'Why?'

She slewed round at the harsh note in his voice, appalled by the grim line of his mouth. Mistrust, doubt, it was all back again. The tautness of his features, the rigidity of his shoulder muscles, the whiteness of the knuckles of the hands that still rested on the steering-wheel, said it all.

But there was nothing she could do about that, not now, difficult though it was to resist the impulse to tell him everything. Or at least enough to allay his doubts of her. There simply wasn't time, and she doubted he would believe her, in any case. Firming her chin, she gave him a long steady look.

'All I ask is five minutes alone with Claudia. I— her initial reaction to the news might have her saying things she'd regret later. She's grown to rely on me since—just lately.'

'Or you on her? She's the living link with your late husband, isn't she?' he questioned tightly and Tiah searched his bleak features with troubled eyes, loving him yet holding so much back. Ashamed of doing so.

'Just five minutes,' she repeated, adding with fierce immediacy, 'I've said I'll marry you. And it's you and I who will be relying on each other for a long time to come. Hopefully. Claudia doesn't come into it.'

She left the car, knowing he would give her the time she needed, her shoulders unconsciously squaring as she walked through the front door.

Polly was dusting the furniture and she had one of Oliver's silver-framed photographs in her hands and she glanced up, smiling, when Tiah greeted her, not one whit put out by her strange mode of dress.

'Where's Claudia?' Tiah asked, hoping she didn't

sound as apprehensive as she felt, and Polly jerked her head.

'In the sitting-room. Brooding. I don't know what's got into her now. She tries my patience sometimes, she does.'

That didn't augur well and Tiah was thankful she had asked for five minutes' grace. Claudia could well say some dreadful things, and Lucas had been hurt enough by what he believed to be her own reluctance to let go of Oliver's memory.

She pushed her hands deep into the pockets of the old gardening coat which had been the first thing she had grabbed when Lucas had ordered her out of here last night, and walked quickly across the hall.

Claudia was at the table in front of the window. She, too, was still wearing the dress she had worn for the dinner party last night. But, unlike Tiah, she didn't look as though she had been to bed at all.

Tiah cleared her throat edgily, 'Claudia——' and the older woman looked up, her dark eyes sunk into her head. There was a polished walnut box on the table in front of her and there were various papers scattered around.

'So you've come home at last.' The voice was harsh, grating, so unlike her normal smooth tones that Tiah gave an involuntary shudder. 'You spent the night with that Clent man. He told me. I only hope we can keep it from Oliver.'

Tiah's stomach twisted with deep instinctive fear. But she made herself go forward, compassion the stronger emotion. She took Claudia's hands and they felt dry and cold and bony, like a bundle of dead twigs and leaves, and Tiah drew in a shuddering breath between ashen lips.

'Claudia—I am going to marry Lucas. We love each other, please try to understand.'

'Marry Lucas Clent!' The frail hands were dragged from Tiah's grasp. 'You must be mad! You are Oliver's wife! Lucas Clent is an evil man. I didn't want to show you this before. I have to, now. Look——'

The long white hands seemed to take on a manic life of their own as they scrabbled among the papers remaining in the box, eventually producing a faded sheet of newsprint.

'Read this. Read it—it will show you exactly the type of man your precious Lucas Clent is!'

The breath solidified in Tiah's chest, hurting her, her heart battering against her ribs. If Lucas came in and saw poor Claudia as she was now, no explanations would be needed. That his seeing her this way would be degrading to the older woman no longer seemed to matter as much as it had done. Claudia was beyond thinking rationally now.

Reluctantly, Tiah took the paper, not knowing what to expect, not caring much. And because she needed to keep Claudia calm, relatively so anyway, she scanned the print. It was a review page from the *Gazette*, dated a few months before Tiah had met Oliver. Lucas would have taken over the paper by then, following his father's death, and obviously, because of his experience with his American arts magazine, he had taken over the art reviews for the *Gazette*.

There was a photograph of Oliver, blurred, indistinct. A headline: 'Local artist stages exhibition in Priory grounds,' and the following hundred odd words were a calm dissection of his work. Words like 'pretentious' and 'facile' set the faintly denigrating tone and Tiah put the paper down on the table, her shoulders sagging.

So this was why Claudia had loathed the very idea of Lucas from the start, why she had been so much against Tiah's exhibition, been driven to sneak one of Oliver's paintings in with Tiah's work. It had been jealousy, bitterness because Oliver's work had been badly reviewed by the very man who had thought Tiah's work good enough to be shown.

'Oliver was a genius,' Claudia spat. 'Lucas Clent's father had refused him space at that hateful little gallery—Oliver's work was too good, we both knew that. It would have shown everything else up for the amateurish rubbish it was. Then the old man died,' she made a thick noise in her throat. 'But by that time Oliver had arranged his own exhibition. And Lucas Clent went and wrote those lies. He was jealous of Oliver's talent. And now he's trying to take you away from Oliver because he's jealous of your beautiful marriage.' Her voice rose, her eyes narrowing to glittering, furious slits. 'And you are letting him!'

Swaying, Tiah reached out to the older woman. 'Claudia, please—Oliver died, he——'

'I shall stop it!' Tears were raining down the ravaged old face and Tiah froze. She had never seen Claudia cry before. Even at Oliver's funeral she had remained dry-eyed, calm, completely in control. 'I shall put a stop to it, do you hear?' The trembling mouth worked piteously. 'That evil man hurt him before with his poisonous lies. I won't let him hurt him again!'

She staggered to the door, her arms outstretched, like a sleepwalker, or a mother searching for her lost child, Tiah thought defeatedly, letting her go.

The precarious balance was no longer held. There was no way Tiah could walk out and leave her.

She felt cold, right through to the innermost tissues of her being and her heart punched her ribs as Lucas appeared in the doorway, tall and lithe and vital, his eyes searching her ashy white face. He walked towards her, steadily, his mouth tightening, his eyes questioning.

'Tiah?'

'I am so sorry——' she gestured helplessly. 'I can't walk out on Claudia now.' She was going to have to tell him the truth, or part of it. 'Our marriage will have to wait until you get back from America.' She would need time, time to get Claudia to a doctor, to see her settled into a private nursing home where she could be professionally cared for. There was no way she could turn her back on her responsibilities, walk out, marry Lucas tomorrow and fly to New York with him.

'No!' His voice was a hard denial. 'I won't leave you here. What changed your mind, dammit?'

She shrugged helplessly, searching for the words to explain Claudia's sickness, her eyes misting.

'It's Claudia—she——'

'Claudia, hell!' He exploded raggedly, cutting into her fumbling words, reaching the limits of his endurance. And suddenly he tensed, his body growing still as his hand slowly reached out, like a slow-motion sequence in dream time, to fasten on the sheet of newsprint.

His eyes swept it dispassionately, then rose to hold hers in a blank stare, only the glittering points of light in the sombre pupils denoting what was going on in his head.

'I see. This.' The paper dropped to the floor, and he pushed his hands into the pockets of his

trousers, his powerful shoulders bunched, massive.
'I had no personal axe to grind. I wrote the truth.
Oliver's work was a sham. If anything, I minced
my words when I wrote that piece. It has nothing
to do with either of us. Oliver is over and done
with. Dead. Gone. And Tiah,' his eyes bored deep
into her soul, shrivelling it, his voice, cool deadly
and calculating, compounding her misery, 'come
with me. Now. Marry me tomorrow, or never. I'm
not begging, I'm giving you that choice. All I ask
is that you think very carefully before you make
it.'

Tiah stared at him, horrified. He meant it. Now
or never. Her heart tapped its own urgent message
and a thousand jumbled words battered at her
brain. But the only two to get past her constricted
throat had him turning on his heels, not looking
back.

'I can't!'

The room seemed very empty after he had gone.
Very silent. Oliver's photographed eyes stared at
her, mocking, infinitely knowing.

Lucas hadn't given her the opportunity to explain.
He had issued his ultimatum and left. It was all
over.

Tiah ground her small white teeth together, rage
getting through, bringing her alive again. He could
have given her the opportunity to explain, damn
him!

But if he had stayed, just long enough for her to
tell him why she couldn't leave Claudia now, would
things have been any different?

She would never know, and defeat dragged her
down. She loved Lucas, always would, but she had
to look after Claudia now. She had no choice.
Because if Oliver hadn't died, Claudia would still

be the contented, sane woman she had always been. Over-possessive, maybe, but sane.

If Oliver had lived. But he hadn't. She, Tiah, had been responsible for his death. That type of guilt was hard to live with, and it made her responsible for Claudia now. Forever.

Slowly, her grief and responsibility lying heavily on her, the loss of Lucas a painful wound she didn't know how she would ever come to terms with, she moved to the door. She had to go to Claudia, see what could be done. Find Polly, phone the doctor. And as she crossed the hall, beneath the watchful painted eyes, the haunting strains of *Danse Macabre* enveloped her, sealing her empty future.

CHAPTER TEN

'SHE's going to be all right.' Polly came out of Claudia's room, closing the door softly behind her.

'How can you be so sure? I think we ought to contact Doctor Fletcher.' Tiah's mouth formulated the words with difficulty. Her lips felt stiff. Dead. She felt dead all over, had done—except for that brief flash of anger—since Lucas had walked out.

'There's no need for that. She's sleeping peacefully, poor lamb.'

Polly pushed her face closer, her little black eyes peering up at Tiah from beneath the brim of yet another odd hat. The unlit corridor was gloomy, the rain-drenched atmosphere permeating to the heart of the silent old house. Everything was gloomy, the long-term prognosis no better.

'You look like death,' Polly pronounced sourly. 'Come down to the kitchen and I'll make us a cup of tea.'

'But Claudia?' Tiah gestured stiffly to the closed door. It could have been ten minutes, or an hour, since Lucas had walked away from her. Tiah had no way of knowing. Half way up the stairs her knees had given way and she had sat there, hunched, her bright head in her hands, looking at the cold hard face of loss, until she could bear it no longer, could understand nothing of the dreadful reason behind it all. The music had stopped by then and she had hauled herself upright again, on her way to find her demented sister-in-law.

'I told you.' Polly stumped away down the corridor. 'She's asleep and will be all right and there's no need for you to look like the world's blown up in your face. So I'll make that tea. Come on.'

'Yes,' Tiah answered dully. 'But I'll change first. I won't be long.' Her world *had* blown up, disintegrating into a pile of ashes.

In her room, the little blue room where she had once felt so secure, she moved like an automaton, hanging the stained old gardening coat on a peg on the door, taking the glittering emerald eardrops from the pockets where she had put them last night for safe keeping. Last night—when she and Lucas, as innocent as children, had slept in each other's arms, seemed a lifetime away. Something that would never be repeated, never be forgotten.

Was her whole life to be spent in the past? Were isolated fragments of time gone by the only things left to her? Listlessly, she removed the jade dress and dropped it heedlessly to the floor, pulling on grey tailored trousers and a scarlet sweater. The vibrant colour made her face look paper-white. She looked spineless and defeated, a thing of no substance, and she hated herself.

And all this mess was her own fault. If she had told Lucas, when she had first discovered that she loved him, of Claudia's mental state—or if she hadn't been responsible for Oliver's death in the first place, felt the guilt so keenly, then none of this would have happened.

But it had happened, and she had to live with the future, as she had made it, so she had better make a start right now and try to pull herself together.

The hot tea helped a little. At least, it warmed her, although it didn't reach the cold spot, deep inside her. That, she supposed, with the resignation of utter despair, was something she would have to learn to live with, too.

'I was walking through the hall when she came stumbling through,' Polly recounted, stirring the fourth spoonful of sugar into her tea. 'I knew something was up—she looked half crazy. So I followed her up the stairs—muttering away, she was. And she went to her room and put a tape of that horrid music on that player thing she's got up there. She didn't seem to know what she was doing so I put her to bed—crying like a baby she was. Then I switched that music off, and do you know what she did?' A great satisfied grin cracked Polly's face and Tiah, dropping her eyes, tracing the pattern of the red-checked tablecloth with the unsteady tip of a finger, wondered what in the world there was to smile about.

'She suddenly sat up in bed,' Polly told her, undeterred by the lack of interest, 'and said, as clear as crystal, "Oliver's gone. He's dead and I'm all alone." And I said, "Yes, he's gone, but you're not alone. You've got me." And she cried some more, quietly, like, and I held her hand while she dropped off to sleep.'

'Earlier, she'd been talking as though he were still alive,' Tiah said heavily, unable to share Polly's optimism. 'It was horrible. She's been getting worse over the last few months.' There was a loose thread on the cloth, scarlet, like a thread of blood, and she picked at it listlessly, and Polly said, 'I know, I've seen it coming. It had to happen—on account of the way she sort of carried on as normal after he died. It was as if she couldn't let go, weep as anyone else would, because she wouldn't have known how to cope with that much sorrow. Only it will be all right now. She's let herself admit that he's gone. She won't get up to her crazy nonsense again.'

'I told her Lucas and I were getting married,' Tiah explained. 'She went over the top.'

'And came down with a bump on the other side,' Polly commented sagely, stacking the cups and carrying them over to the sink. 'And a good job, too. So, when's the wedding? I *do* like that young man.'

'The wedding's off.' Saying it aloud made it seem more real, more immediate, and Tiah saw Polly through a haze of tears as the older woman turned from the sink, her hands on her hips, glaring.

'Off? And why?'

'Because——' Tiah shrugged, the effort almost too much, and gave a brief account of his ultimatum, her reasons for refusing, and Polly snorted,

'Well, what are you sitting there for—picking holes in a perfectly good tablecloth! Get over to his place. Smartish. If the wedding's tomorrow morning, you'll need to get things sorted out today. Don't just sit there!'

'I can't. I——'

'Can't or won't?' Polly snapped. 'Your reasons for staying with Claudia were all very well and good at the time. Now they're not. She's going to be all right, or my name's not Polly Banks. I can see to her. No call for you to do a thing. She'll be a bit down for a week or two—stands to reason. But she'll get over that.'

'How could you manage her?' Tiah asked wearily and Polly echoed crossly,

'Manage? *How!* I've been managing Miss Claudia since she was in nappies! You go and make it up with your man. And don't worry, I'll stay here with her and as soon as she's feeling stronger I'll tell her to come and stay along with me for a bit. After that, we'll have to see. I might even persuade her to leave this nasty spooky old place for good.'

Tiah doubted that. Claudia was firmly rooted here. She said to Polly, 'I once asked you if you would consider living-in here. You refused. You wouldn't want to have to sleep here now, you know you wouldn't.'

'No bother,' Polly stared at Tiah as if she were particularly dense. 'That was then. This is now. Oliver isn't here now, she's let him go.' Then, tutting, 'Cut along and sort yourself out with your man, do!'

Tiah got to her feet. Arguing with Polly wouldn't achieve a thing. And Lucas had meant it when he'd said now or never. As far as he was concerned she had chosen never.

'I'll just look in on Claudia.'

She was still sleeping, the lines of strain magically erased from her face, and Tiah sat in an armchair near the bed and stared at nothing, her mind wandering. Lucas couldn't have loved her deeply if he'd been prepared to issue an ultimatum such as that. The thought tormented her, wandering around the corridors of her mind until she thought she would go mad with it. And then, out of nowhere, her mind cleared. He *must* have loved her. He had loved her, wanted to marry her, despite his belief that everything she did or said was governed by her love for a man who was dead. He had even believed that her sudden change of mind regarding the wedding date she'd already agreed to had been triggered by the newspaper cutting. And still he had given her the opportunity to become his wife. He had been willing to take that chance, hoping, believing, that married to him she would forget the past, grow to love him as he loved her.

She had never told him she loved him, never contradicted the wrong impressions he had gained. So he must have loved her deeply, with true generosity.

It had only been when he had offered her a clear-cut choice, and she had—as far as he was concerned—taken the wrong one, that he had finally and completely washed his hands of her.

And that was because—her mind was totally clear now—and she began to pace the room, recalling something Ellie had said: 'He rejected me as I rejected him. He has never forgiven me for making the only choice I could.'

Would he ever forgive her? Tiah thought distractedly. Could he? He had once told her that his parents' break-up hadn't affected him. But it had, even if he didn't know it. He had overheard his father giving his mother the choice—her husband and her son, or her lover. She had chosen her lover, and Lucas had been aware of that choice. He had been rejected at a particularly vulnerable age, and it had scarred him more than he knew. So maybe he wouldn't be capable of forgiveness.

But Tiah hoped he was, her desperation bringing beads of sweat to slick her forehead, dampen her palms. To find out she would have to go to him.

Beg him, if need be, to allow the wedding to go ahead tomorrow. She had to try.

She paused at the foot of the bed. Claudia was still sleeping like a baby. It would be a pity to wake her. But Tiah couldn't walk out without a word. Moving forward, soft-footed, she gently shook the sleeping woman's shoulder, aware, from the quiet snick of the door behind her, that Polly had come into the room. No sound but that of Claudia's regular breathing, the little mew in her throat as she woke, turning her head on the pillow, her eyes moving slowly from Tiah to Polly and back again.

'Claudia——' Tiah took the long pale hand that rested on the counterpane. 'Polly is going to stay here with you, but I'm going to find Lucas. And if he'll still have me, I'm going to marry him. Tomorrow. Do you understand?'

The slight answering pressure of the thin hand, the sudden welling of tears that glistened in the steady dark eyes, gave Tiah the answer she had been looking for. Claudia was herself again. She was here, in the present, no longer imprisoned by the past. For Claudia, living in the present would be painful, Tiah knew, and her glance slid sideways to Polly.

'You be sure you send us a postcard from New York, Miss Tiah.' Polly bustled forward, fussing with Claudia's pillows. 'You'll be back in time for Christmas, didn't you say?'

Lucas had said he would be back then, but whether Tiah would be with him, as his wife, she had no way of telling. But she understood what Polly was trying to do, and nodded, forcing a smile.

'There now, Miss Claudia—won't that be something to look forward to? We'll all be together for a nice old-fashioned Christmas—like in the old days. Sit up a little, dear—that's right. Now I'm going to bring our lunch up—a nice piece of plaice—and we'll both have it here, from trays. Then you can have another little rest while I make a bed up for myself in the next room. And tomorrow, if it's fine, I'll drive you over to see my cottage. You haven't seen it since I moved in, have you? I know you'll like it—but my, the garden's a mess. I'm no hand when it comes to making a garden out of a sea of nettles. But you could suggest what we could do with it—make the plans and so on—and Joe can do the rough——'

Tiah left them, slipping down the corridor to her own room. Not allowing herself to think how bleak her future would be if Lucas refused to listen to her, she pulled a small suitcase from the back of the wardrobe and rummaged through her clothing, wondering what to take.

She threw in a couple of nightgowns, underwear, then, impatient with her indecision, bundled up the pale yellow skirt-suit Claudia had made her for her birthday, and tossed it into the case, following it with a dark grey silk blouse. The outfit would double for the wedding and the flight to New York. If there was to be a wedding . . .

Hurriedly, she found her passport and other essential documents, tossed them on top of the clothes and zipped the case shut. If she started to think of the horribly real possibility that there might not be a wedding at all she would lose what little courage she had and give up. Stay exactly where she was.

Reaching Compton, she parked as close to the

Gazette offices as she could get and walked the short distance, oblivious of the rain that soaked through her sweater and slacks, feeling sick with nerves. What if he refused to see her, told her to get lost, that he had had enough, had decided he didn't want to marry her and the ghost of her dead husband? What if he didn't give her the chance to explain? He had given her no opportunity at all this morning—so why should he relent now? He had done enough comprising in the past, heaven knew. And that ultimatum of his, when his patience, his tolerance, had suddenly deserted him, had been very final.

Her thoughts drained what little colour she had left in her face and she had to summon all her willpower to get herself through the revolving glass doors.

Disorientated, Tiah approached the reception desk where two women were kept busy answering queries, taking in small ads, and she joined the short queue, suddenly shivering.

From behind a glass partition came the clatter of typewriters, the shrill of a telephone, muted voices, and Tiah shuffled forwards, blinking distractedly at a pert young woman whose mouth, as she said, 'Good morning, may I help?' seemed to twitch with amusement.

'I—er——' Tiah's voice seemed to have got stuck in her throat and she swallowed hard, trying to get a grip on herself. 'I'd like to see Mr Clent, please, Lucas Clent.'

'Do you have an appointment?' The receptionist's slanting eyebrows rose by a quiver as she ran the tip of a painted nail down a line of squiggles in a diary, and Tiah said no, she hadn't, but thought he would see her, in any case.

'Mr Clent is tied up all day.' The cold green eyes stated that even if he weren't she wouldn't let her past, not without an appointment. 'If you'd like to leave your name, I'll see if I can fit you in to see our assistant manager some time next week.'

Shaking her head, Tiah turned away, only now conscious of how she must look—wet hair hanging in rats' tails down her back, sodden clothes, anxious lost eyes . . . No wonder the receptionist hadn't even troubled to lift the phone to ask if he would make time to see her.

She would have liked to be able to speak to him, to judge his reaction when she promised full explanations. It would have made the lonely waiting hours easier to bear. Shrugging, she squelched back through the rain to her car and drove out of town to his flat.

At least she still had his key and could let herself in and wait. But the silent rooms held no comfort. The bed, where they had slept together last night, had been stripped. She knew he hadn't done it first thing this morning, so he must have returned here, after walking away from her, making time in his busy day to clear away every last trace of her. His priorities flattened her.

But hovering around, shivering with cold and anxiety, wasn't doing her any good and she made a determined effort to pull herself together. He had said he would be back at seven. She looked at her watch. Five hours to go. She could at least occupy them usefully.

Stripping her wet clothes off, she put them in the dryer, the ordinary, everyday sound of its mumbling chug settling her mind a little. Naked, she padded to the bathroom she had used last night and ran hot water, and later, wrapped in a navy blue bath sheet, warm again, she found the ironing board and pressed the suit and blouse she had bundled into her case, hanging them in the empty wardrobe in the room she had used. That done, she took her clothes from the dryer and pulled them on and made herself a pot of tea. Still three hours to go.

But she was beginning to feel better, more confident. She would have a meal ready for seven; she had found the steaks, salad things, in the fridge, and surely, finding her here, he would at least do her the courtesy of listening to what she had to say.

At ten past seven she had laid the table in the long sitting-room, making it as attractive as she could. She had been out, buying wine and a fresh French loaf, and the prepared salad was in a bowl in the fridge, the wine uncorked, the steak gently grilling. She had made up her face with care, brushed her hair until it shone like spun light and was as ready as she would ever be to face him.

At ten past eight, her ears aching from straining to hear the sound of his key in the door, she dialled the number of the *Gazette*, was answered by one of the night staff, and was told that Mr Clent had left an hour ago.

So where was he? Phoning Polly, on the vague off-chance that he might have relented enough to drive over to Deepdene, she learned that he had not. Claudia, though, she was informed, was bearing up wonderfully, grieving for Oliver, but naturally this time, and already showing an interest in seeing Polly's cottage, particularly the neglected garden.

Which was good. Very good. And Tiah was glad. But it didn't explain where Lucas was. Sudden, violent apprehension had her running down the corridor, looking for his room. Flinging the door wide, she sagged with relief. A suitcase stood at the foot of the bed, and a flight bag. So he hadn't as she had so suddenly feared, taken an earlier flight to New York.

At midnight she knew he wouldn't be coming back until it was time to pick up his luggage. Ellie had spoken of his other 'lady-friends'. He had probably decided to spend what should have been his wedding eve consoling himself with one of them.

Miserable to the point of repacking her case and driving back to Deepdene, Tiah realised that she didn't even have the spirit to do that. Turning off the warming oven—the steaks had been ruined beyond redemption hours ago—she dragged herself back to the sitting-room, and poured herself a glass of wine.

Curling up in a corner of the wide sofa she sipped the wine slowly. She had eaten nothing since breakfast with Lucas. How wonderful everything had seemed then. How neatly they had made their plans, how warmly, lovingly, he had looked at her. And later, how coldly, when a few traumatic moments of time, a handful of stark, ungiving words, had shattered all their hopes.

Her eyes filled with aching, burning tears and she gulped the remains of the wine in her glass. Later, when she felt more in control, she would bow to the inevitable and get herself back to Deepdene. Where her future lay, she couldn't tell and couldn't summon the enthusiasm to think about it . . .

When she woke she had no idea how long she had slept, she only knew, without opening her eyes, that Lucas was in the room with her. She murmured his name, the sound catching in her throat, lifting heavy lashes.

He was standing over her and how long he had been there she had no way of telling. But by the light of the single table lamp she had left burning she could read the weariness, the strain on his face.

'Lucas——' She reached out a hand, uncurling herself, coming fully awake, but he backed away, the movement decisive.

Hurt, frightened by this stark evidence of what had happened to them, she watched as he swung away, his shoulders taut with tension as he poured brandy into a glass. And his voice was thick, slurred, as if he had already had more to drink than was wise.

'I don't know what you're doing here, but I'm asking you to leave. There's a limit to the amount of torment I can take. Beyond that, and I'm burned out.'

It sounded so final, as if she had killed his love as surely as she had killed Oliver. But she knew she would never again have the opportunity to tell him she loved him. She had never been able to tell him before. Admitting it would have laid her open to so much that was painful. But that didn't signify now. She had already lost everything there was to lose.

Straightening her legs, she stood up unsteadily, her eyes on the unresponsive back of his head.

'I'll go. I came to tell you that I love you.'

The words dropped like chips of glass into crystal water, their meaning plain. But he seemed not to hear, or to care, and she reached blindly for the shoes she had discarded earlier, her fingers freezing to utter stillness as he bit out, 'For how long will you "love" me! Until the next time I ask you to fix a date for a wedding? And then the next—and the next?' He twisted round to face her, the brandy slopping from the glass he clutched, his knuckles white. 'I don't play second fiddle to any man— certainly not a bloody ghost!'

His vehemence, his ravaged eyes, gave her hope. He cared, he still cared, and it was eating him up inside. She wanted to go to him, to hold him, but knew that if she did his control would shatter. He would thrust her away, instinctively, using his physical strength to protect his heart and mind from further hurt.

Knowing she had to control herself far more rigorously than she had ever been called on to do before—or lose this last forlorn little hope—she walked to the table and poured herself more wine, sheer willpower keeping her hands steady.

'I thought you were leaving,' he rasped, his hand tightening round the glass he held until she was afraid he would crush it, spilling the contents, his blood, along with his pain.

'So I am—in a moment.' She sipped the wine, not wanting it, but it gave her something to do. 'I wanted you to know that after Oliver died I promised myself that I would never marry again.'

If she had to tell him everything, then she had to start at the beginning. But the beginning went way back, beyond the point of his death. Her head began to throb in time with the pattering beat of her heart, and Lucas snapped, white-lipped, 'So? What's new? He was so perfect, wasn't he? Too perfect for his place to be usurped by any other man! But you're young, you're beautiful, you have normal sexual needs. You might lust after sex with another man, but that's as far as it goes. Marriage is out. No man will ever be allowed to take that place—*his* place, in your life again. Well, I'm not going to be used as a stud. So you may as well leave right now!'

'Fair enough.' It was an effort, dear God it was an effort to keep hold of herself. Drawing a breath in through her pale lips, she schooled her voice to impassivity. 'If you will listen, instead of leaping to conclusions, you'll learn that I swore never to marry again because I wasn't willing to lay myself open to that kind of hurt. Not again. And I don't mean the pain of bereavement, as you so wrongly suppose.'

She crossed to the sofa and sank down, feet carefully placed together, the shaking of her hands subdued to the merest tremor. He half turned, and she responded to the respite of his slight interest, the query in his eyes. 'I had been a year in my first job when I met Oliver. I worked in a shop selling artists' materials—in Cheltenham. Had a bed-sitter, one or two not very close friends. Oliver was staying in the area, he came into the shop. He told me, later, that he had fallen in love with me at once. It seemed romantic at the time—this obsession he seemed to have with me. No one else had ever loved me. It was a new thing for me because not even my own parents had loved or wanted me. Later, I came to realise that it had been a certain kind of gratitude that had made me agree to marry him, believe I loved him.'

'Believe?'

It was the first word he had uttered since she had sensed the beginning of his interest, the lessening of his need to see the back of her. She caught it up, reiterating strongly, 'Yes. *Believe*.' She gathered a deep breath. 'He was good-looking, wealthy, talented—or so he continually told me. What counted most, though, for me, was his home, his beautiful home complete with a ready-made mother/sister substitute. I had never had a home, or a sister, or—to all practical intents—a mother. Had never received love. All these were there, ready and waiting for me at Deepdene. And so I married him, mistaking gratitude and fondness for love. I was totally

innocent. Oliver had never tried to get me to bed
with him before we were married. I thought, at the
time, it was because he respected me.'

Tiah finished her wine and clutched her empty
glass in nervously twisting fingers. This was the hard
part, the part she had never spoken to anyone about.
The memory shamed her, degraded her. But if Lucas
was ever to believe that he need fear no adverse
comparisons with the man who had been her
husband, she had to go on.

'And?' Lucas moved towards her, panther-like.
He took the glass from her hands, his eyes shadowed.
'More wine?'

She shook her head and he sat beside her, leaning
back against the opposite corner of the long sofa.
And she plunged on, knowing that, for his sake, she
had to break through to the place in her mind that
she had so carefully blocked out.

'Oliver loved me. There was never any doubt of
that. But his ways of loving were not——' her voice
faltered and she raised pleading, drowning eyes to
him, a silent plea for permission to let things lie. But
his voice compelled her, 'Go on. His ways of
loving——?'

'He was impotent.' The words, the memories that
she had blanked out, only reliving in the dreams that
sometimes came to haunt her, tore at her. 'He
wanted to make love to me. But he couldn't. At first
he used to break down and weep, and I would tell
him it didn't matter, that maybe things would get
better. But later, he came to blame me. He forced
me to do degrading things. Shaming things—to—to
excite him enough to—ah, Lucas!' She buried her
bright head in her hands, her slender body shaking
with the unbearable pressure of memories. Memories

she had blanked out of her mind, surfacing only in her worst dreams.

'Tiah,' his voice was thick, the hand that stroked her down-bent head gentle. 'Why didn't you tell me?'

'I couldn't!' A convulsive shudder ripped through her but he continued to stroke her hair, soothing, calming, gentling her, the way he might any frightened creature. But at last she was able to go on, 'After he died I did my damnedest to forget those—those dark things. I remembered only the good—the home he had given me, the affection of his sister who had become like a mother to me. Claudia never knew of the dark side of our marriage. She only knew that her beloved Oliver loved me, that I made a welcome addition to her little family. She sometimes spoke of the children Oliver and I would one day have—not knowing. And after it was over I didn't have the heart to tell her, to spoil her memories of him.'

'Why did you stay?' His question was quiet, underscored with bitterness, and she leaned back against the sofa, her closed eyes bruised, trembling.

'In the beginning, I thought it might get better, that his impotency might not last. Apart from that, I was happier than I had ever been. And then, when things got worse, when he began to drink secretly, make me do things that degraded me, I realised I couldn't take any more, that things would only get worse. I stuck it for as long as I could, because I had married him for better or worse. Finally, I had to go. I told him. I packed a few things. Late at night.'

Behind closed eyelids she could see again the rage that had possessed him. Hear the obscene words as she had abandoned her half-packed suitcase and clattered down the stairs, away from him. Running down the stairs, hearing him following, mouthing obscenities in his drunken voice . . .

'I got as far as the foot of the stairs. He was following. But he fell. He was already dying when Claudia came out of her room, disturbed by the noise. I held him, told her to phone for an ambulance. He died in my arms. Poor tormented Oliver.'

She shuddered violently and Lucas reached for her and out of the cold darkness of memory she found his warmth, heard the love in his deep voice, 'Don't think of it. Oh, Tiah, if only you could have told me this before. I went through hell believing that no man could ever compare with him—for you.'

Blindly, she buried her head in his warmth, her hands grasping his body as if she would never let him go, and he bowed his head, his face buried in her hair, his deep voice muffled as he asked, 'Why did you come here? I walked the streets for hours. Left the office to have a bar snack with Don Gates, my assistant manager. He ate, I drank. Left him, walked the streets. Couldn't face the loneliness here. Why did you come?'

He sounded like a man in agony and she answered shakily, 'To ask you to marry me. Tomorrow—as we'd planned,' and she felt him stiffen, his wariness coming through his caring. The fear of yet another rejection would be hard for him to handle. She lifted her head, holding him with her eyes and saw the bleakness in his as he said softly, 'And what makes you believe you can trust another man? How do I know that your understandable instinct for self-preservation—for safety, if you like—won't push everything else to the back of your mind again? Oh, I grant you . . . ' He released her hands carefully, got to his feet. Stood looking down at her. Sorrowful, but rejecting her. 'I grant you that I put the wrong interpretations on your feelings for Oliver all along the line. But the very sight of that old review clipping brought the memories back, had you changing your mind about ever giving yourself—your future—to a man, didn't it?'

'No.' She had to convince him of that. 'I only wanted a stay of execution—oops! Wrong choice of words!' A smile flickered around her mouth at her unthinking gaffe, deepening when she saw the answering light of humour in his indigo eyes. 'Claudia was upset. She'd been unstable since Oliver died. She used to talk as though he was still there, and I was planning to leave him for another man. She was the one who brought all Oliver's canvases in and hung them around the house—his photographs—that music at the dinner table. I wasn't upset because I was reminded of Oliver. It made me ill to know how Claudia's sick mind was working at the time. And this morning, when I told her that you and I were to be married, she—she brought out that cutting. You had hurt Oliver once by writing that article and she, poor sick soul, believed you would hurt him again by marrying me. I couldn't leave her in that state. I knew I'd have things to—to sort out before I could leave her. Hence the request that we postpone the wedding until Christmas. Is it so difficult to trust me, Lucas?'

He rubbed his eyes tiredly and her heart twisted painfully with love for him. She wanted to hold him, to cradle that proud head to her breast, but she knew she had to make him see her strength, her unfailing love for him, with words. With touch, the battle could be too easily won, the victory for ever uncertain.

'I fought against falling in love with you,' she told

him honestly. 'But I gave up that fight. It could produce no winners, only losers. I love you, and I'm trusting my instincts. I know you love me. You gave me a choice, and in your eyes I made the wrong one. You weren't seeing the full picture because I hadn't told you the full truth. I couldn't bring myself to talk about Claudia's mental state. And all I ask now is that you trust me.'

He reached for her then, groaning his need. 'You give me a choice that is no choice. I have to trust you, Tiah. Now, for ever. I love you.'

'Then we marry tomorrow?' Her voice was shaky, but he silenced her, stilled her lips with his until they responded openly, willingly, to the pressure of his and she made a noise in her throat, didn't know whether she was laughing or crying, and he lifted his mouth from hers, his lips moving tantalisingly over her face.

'Why have you been so protective of Claudia? Why didn't you seek outside help long before now?'

'Because I felt guilty. If I hadn't tried to leave, he wouldn't have attempted to follow, wouldn't have fallen to his death. If he hadn't died Claudia would have remained perfectly stable.'

'You have no need to feel guilt over his death,' he told her urgently. 'Promise me you won't?'

Strangely enough, the guilt had been exorcised by Claudia's recovery, and she told him, 'As Oliver died, he said he would never leave me. That wherever I went, he would be there. Claudia heard. And she never openly admitted he was dead—she came to believe those dying words of his.'

'But you didn't.'

Gladly she heard the note of confidence in his voice, and her lips sought his, unconscious of the tears that flooded her face, washing away the past for ever. 'Of course not.' She spoke against his parted lips. 'It was his way of punishing me, even as he died. He promised to haunt me with his kind of love. And in a way, I suppose he succeeded.' She ran the tip of her tongue over his teeth, felt his sudden desire. 'Because until I fell in love with you I was quite content to bury myself away from everyone at Deepdene.'

'But me you couldn't resist!' he spoke teasingly, deliberately lightening the fraught atmosphere, helping her finally to put the dark miasma of the past behind her. Taking the initiative now, he swept her bodily into his arms, carrying her into his bedroom, pushing the door closed behind them with his foot.

'We've both had one hell of a day. And tomorrow—today,' he corrected himself wryly, 'we shall need to look at least half human for our wedding.'

Slowly sliding her down the taut length of his body, he set her on her feet, and she shivered deliciously, aching heat building up inside her, as he began, gently, to undress her, handling her as though she were something precious, fragile.

The last scrap of her clothing removed, he slid her beneath the duvet, his hands going to his tie, removing it, his eyes never leaving her. Watching him undress was the most sensual experience she had ever had. That he was fully aroused, wanting her, was in no doubt at all and she gasped, unable to hide her own longing as he slipped into bed beside her.

'I love you, Tiah,' he murmured throatily, his hands incredible gentle, incredibly sure. 'You are the most precious thing in my life, now and always,' and she turned in his arms, arching against him, her response immediate, setting her on fire. 'Darling,' he said thickly, 'let me make you whole. We're incomplete without each other. Without you I'm less than half a man.'

She woke early, moving lazily, languorously, his infinitely wonderful ways of loving an ecstatic reality. Behind the closed lids of her eyes she could re-live each breathtakingly beautiful sensation, and she snuggled more deeply beneath the duvet, instinctively reaching out for him, finding empty space.

'You have one hour to get ready for your wedding,' his husky voice informed her, and she wriggled round, facing the door, her eyes hazed with love for the man whose sensual promise-filled eyes held hers.

'I've brought you some tea,' he remarked prosaically, setting the cup down on the bedside table, his eyes flicking down as she struggled up against the pillows, the covers sliding back to reveal the pink tipped twin mounds of her naked breasts.

He was wearing a short white towelling robe and his long tanned legs were roughened with dark hair, and Tiah's mouth went dry because she could tell he wanted her again. Now. As she wanted him.

But, demurely, for the sheer enjoyment of teasing him a little, she lowered her lashes, tugging at the duvet to cover herself. Reaching for her tea, a smile tugging at her mouth, she enquired sweetly, 'What have you been doing besides making tea?'

'Showering, and——' He sat on the bed, long sure fingers moving back the covers, exposing the naked, pliant, melting length of her body to his devouring eyes.

'Showering, and——?' she prompted, a croak in her voice as he took the cup from her unresisting hands, her whole body coming alive, each nerve-end on fire, beneath his gaze.

'And telephoning.' His hands moulded her from the breast to thigh and she protested weakly.

'We'll never make it in time for the ceremony if you don't stop doing that. Telephoning who?'

'Ellie.' His hands stilled at the soft curve at the base of her stomach and she gasped, her heavy eyelids closing as intolerable pleasure flooded her. And as his hands began an insidiously sensual exploration she grabbed wildly at her scattered wits, and wriggled with more determination than grace away from the vital temptation to stay exactly where she was, openly inviting him for more of the same.

'Ellie? Oh?' she squeaked as she plopped inelegantly to the floor on the opposite side of the bed, and he grinned down into her hot little face.

'How wise you are, my Tiah! One more second and we'd have lost all hope of being on time for our wedding. Go and get showered and dressed, woman. Before I lose complete control of myself!'

And later, after the ceremony and a celebration lunch, when they returned to his flat, she peeled off her gloves, feeling absurdly shy, the look in her new husband's eyes almost paralysing her with an upsurge of totally wanton desires. She said in a high overbright voice, 'I'm glad you invited Ellie to the wedding,' and one of his eyebrows moved upwards, as if he recognised her stupid shyness, was amused by it.

'Yes. I finally got round to deciding it was time to forgive and forget. I believed you'd rejected me— and if you hadn't had the courage it took to face me and put me right I'd have lost the most precious thing in my life. I realise now that it was no thanks to me that our parting yesterday morning wasn't completely final. Knowing that jolted me into looking at Ellie in a different light. When she and my father split up, in the egocentric way of most children I didn't consider her, or my father. To me, it was I alone who was being held in the balance, weighed and found wanting. In rejecting me, as I saw it then, she made me a loser. And I spent the rest of my life proving to myself I wasn't. But that's all over now,' he told her, his eyes darkening in the look Tiah was coming to know so well. 'I have you, and I don't need to prove a single damn thing.'

His voice had deepened, roughened, and he advanced towards her.

'Shall we drink the champagne I have on ice, wife? Or shall we get an early night, ready for our flight tomorrow?'

Deft fingers were already dealing with the buttons of her suit jacket, her grey silk blouse, and Tiah felt her nipples harden, push against the soft fabric, aching erotically for the touch of his hands. And she reached up and wound her arms around his neck, arching against him.

'Both, husband, would be more than acceptable.'

Harlequin Superromance

Here are the longer, more involving stories you have been waiting for... Superromance.

Modern, believable novels of love, full of the complex joys and heartaches of real people.

Intriguing conflicts based on today's constantly changing life-styles.

Four new titles every month.
Available wherever paperbacks are sold.

Harlequin American Romance

Romances that go one step farther...
American Romance

Realistic stories involving people you can relate to and care about.

Compelling relationships between the mature men and women of today's world.

Romances that capture the core of genuine emotions between a man and a woman.

Join us each month for four new titles wherever paperback books are sold.
Enter the world of American Romance.
